# Merry Christmas Tales

Los Angeles • New York

DreamWorks
STORYTELLERS COLLECTION

# Merry Christmas Tales

DreamWorks Press
Los Angeles · New York

*Especially for Hazel, Myles, and Elsie*

Designed by Laurie Young



First Edition

Printed in China

1 2 3 4 5 6 7 8 9 10

09182014-A-1

ISBN 978-1-941341-01-8

Library of Congress Control Number: 2014939974

Visit dreamworkspress.com

# TABLE OF CONTENTS

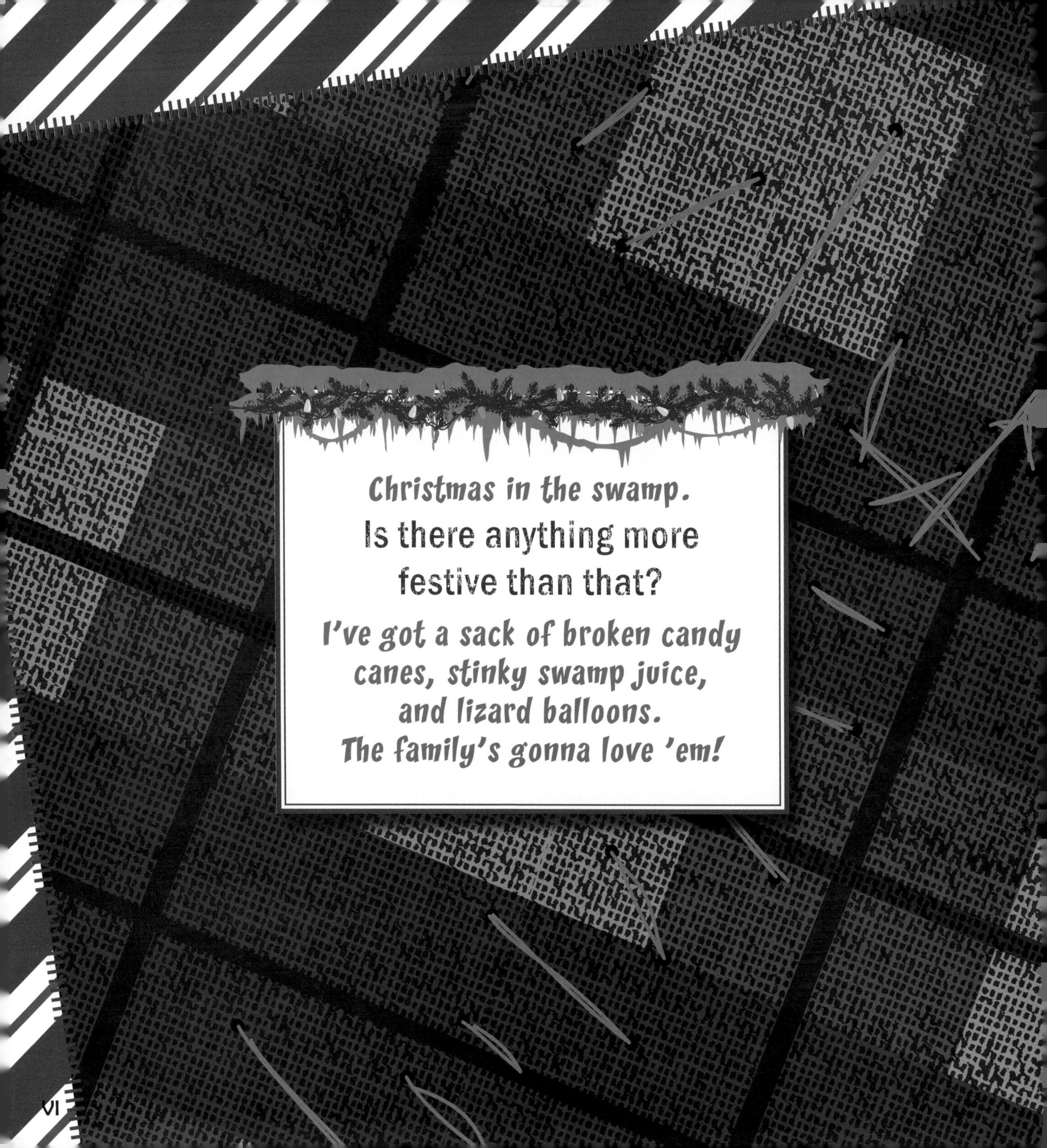
Christmas in the swamp.
Is there anything more festive than that?
I've got a sack of broken candy canes, stinky swamp juice, and lizard balloons.
The family's gonna love 'em!

DreamWorks

# Shrek the Halls

One fine summer day, Shrek finally got his babies down for a nap after watching them play for hours in the mud. Everything was perfect… until Donkey showed up.

"Only one hundred fifty-nine days left till Christmas," Donkey sang out. "So you'd better be good!"

Shrek glared at him. "You'd better be scarce," he said. "I don't care about Christmas."

Yet even as summer turned to fall, Donkey kept reminding Shrek that Christmas was coming.

MERRY ChRIST
Love, DONKEY and FAMILY

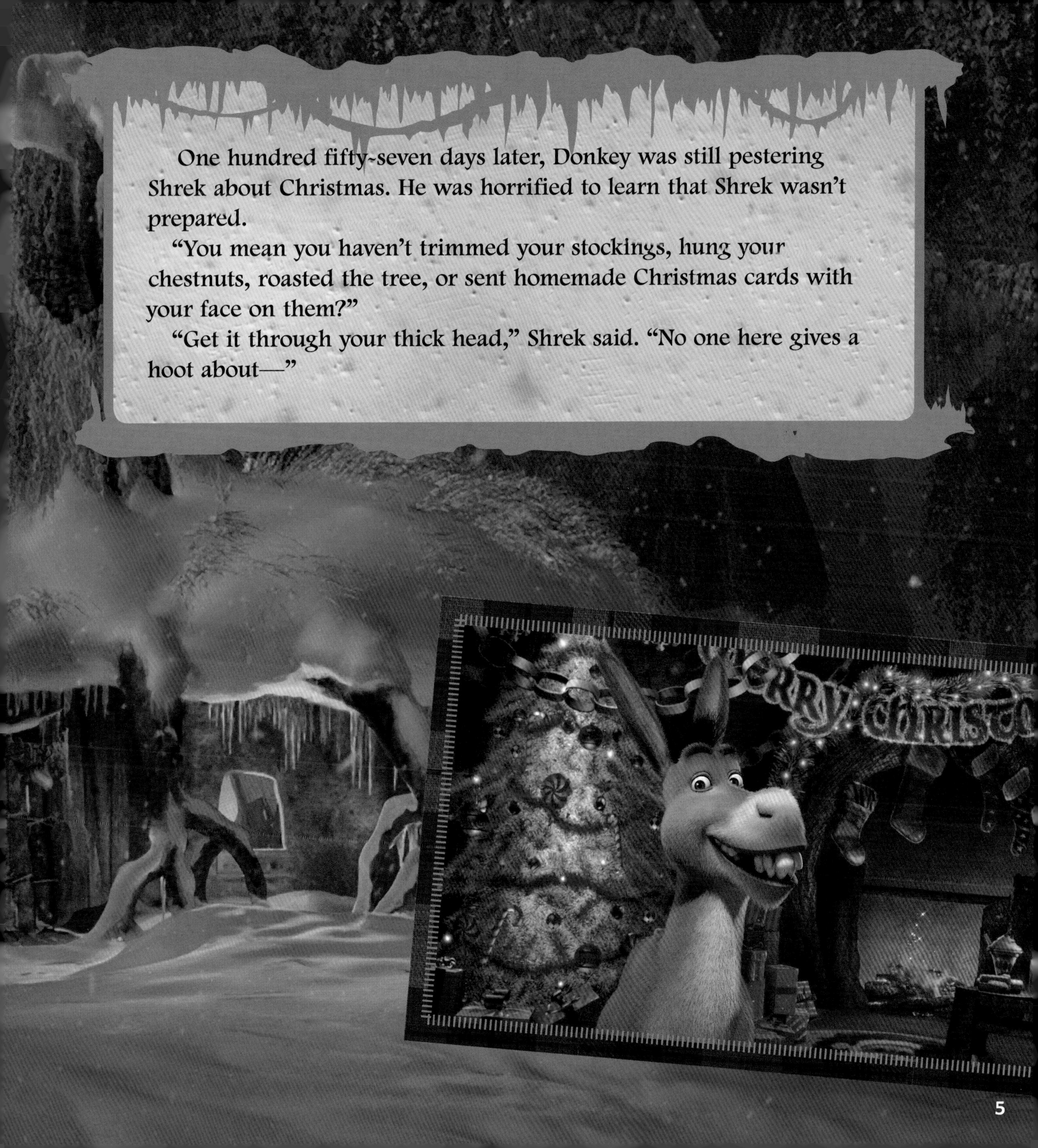

One hundred fifty-seven days later, Donkey was still pestering Shrek about Christmas. He was horrified to learn that Shrek wasn't prepared.

"You mean you haven't trimmed your stockings, hung your chestnuts, roasted the tree, or sent homemade Christmas cards with your face on them?"

"Get it through your thick head," Shrek said. "No one here gives a hoot about—"

Just then, Fiona wandered by with the babies.

"Your first snow!" she cooed happily. "And just in time for Christmas."

Shrek was surprised to see them all so excited. He didn't know the first thing about Christmas! But if it was important to Fiona, it was important to him, too.

CANTERBURY
BOOKS
SORRY WE'RE
CLOSED

That night, he sneaked off to the village bookstore. Luckily, the store had just the book Shrek needed to show him how to have a perfect Christmas.

He just hoped he could pull it off.

Shrek got up early the next morning to decorate the swamp. He didn't have most of the stuff shown in his book, so he had to get creative.

"It's beautiful!" Fiona said when she saw Shrek's decorations.

"It's horrible!" Donkey had just arrived on the scene. "Don't worry, Princess," he told Fiona. "Shrek's going to want my help."

"Actually," Fiona said, "Shrek really wants a nice *family* Christmas."

ONE WAY
NO PARKING

The family set out to gather more decorations.

"This is going to be the best Christmas ever," Fiona said cheerfully. "And we're going to do it together! Now get up and come on!"

They set off into the woods, pulling the babies on a sled. It turned out Fiona could get creative, too! She showed Shrek how to belch on snakes to make them look like candy canes. The babies even helped by blowing up lizard balloons.

Soon, they had found plenty of decorations.

Finally, the house looked almost like the pictures in Shrek's book.

"It's perfect," Shrek said with relief as he and his family relaxed in front of the fire. "And now, it's story time.

"'Twas the night before Christmas, and all through the house . . .'"

The door burst open. "Merry Christmas, Shrek!" Donkey cried.

He rushed in, followed by all the fairy-tale friends.

CHRISTMAS FOR VILLAGE IDIOTS

"Feliz Navidad!" Puss in Boots shouted, doing a Christmas jig.

"Nice to see you, Fiona," one of the Three Little Pigs added.

Greetings filled the house as more and more friends swarmed in.

"What a nice surprise!" Fiona exclaimed.

"Oh, yeah," Shrek grumbled.

He couldn't believe it—his perfect family Christmas had just turned into a crazy, crowded party!

Shrek tried to sneak away to tell his babies their Christmas story, but Donkey overheard.

"Are you telling The Night Before Christmas?" he shouted. "I tell it better than anybody! Gather 'round, everybody."

Donkey recited a wild version about a big Christmas parade and a fifty-foot Santa made of waffles.

Gingy interrupted, looking upset. "Where I come from, Christmas is a nightmare!" he cried. He told a scary story about a giant, hungry Santa.

Shrek had had enough. This was not how he'd planned his perfect family Christmas!

**"Out!"** he yelled. **"I want everybody out of my house right now!"**

Donkey was thrown out the window and landed with a splat. The rest of the fairy-tale friends hurried out behind him.

"Nice way to treat your guests on Christmas, Ebenezer Shrek!" Donkey huffed. "If you think I'm going to give you a present now, you're *sadly* mistaken!"

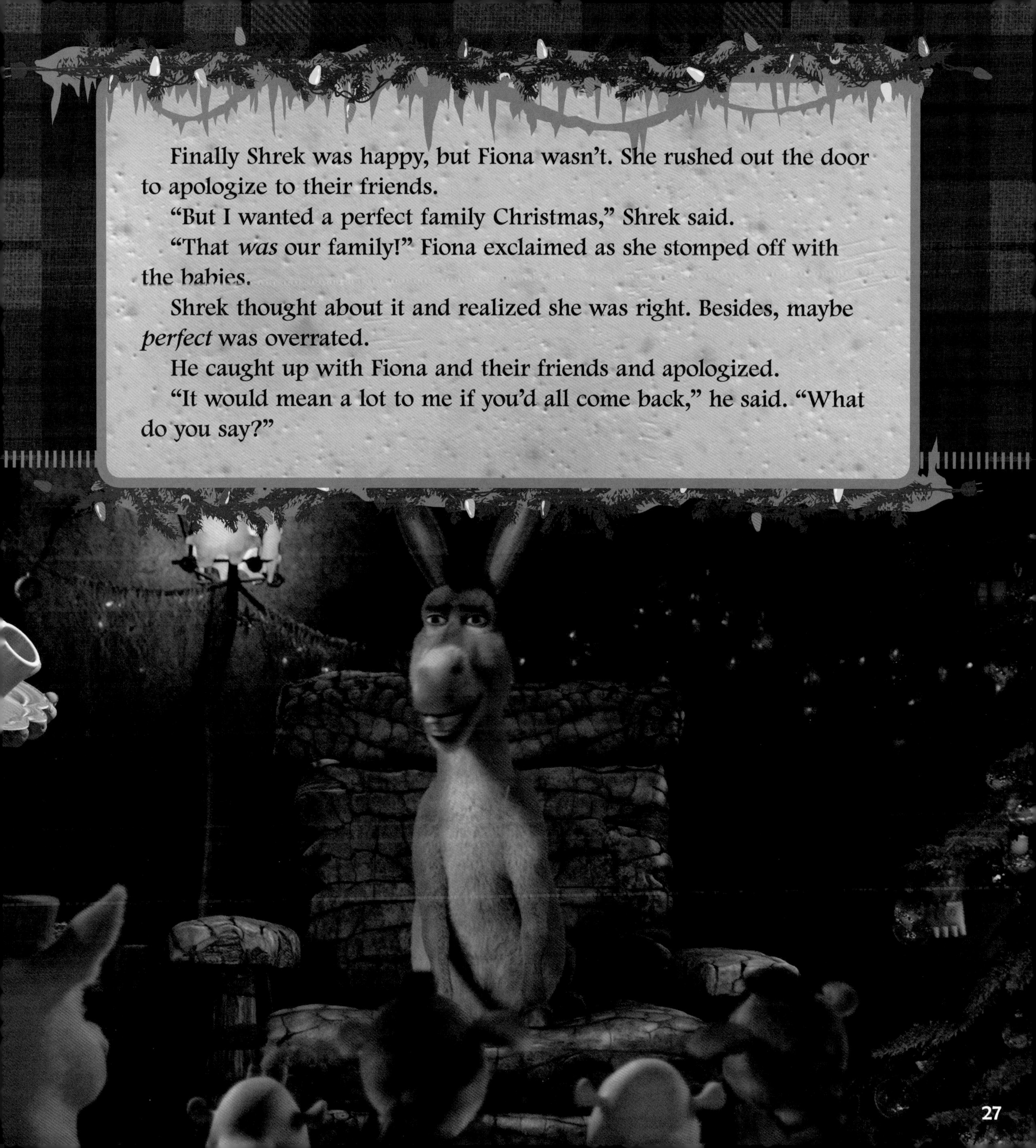

Finally Shrek was happy, but Fiona wasn't. She rushed out the door to apologize to their friends.

"But I wanted a perfect family Christmas," Shrek said.

"That *was* our family!" Fiona exclaimed as she stomped off with the babies.

Shrek thought about it and realized she was right. Besides, maybe *perfect* was overrated.

He caught up with Fiona and their friends and apologized.

"It would mean a lot to me if you'd all come back," he said. "What do you say?"

CHRISTMAS
VILLAGE IDIOTS

Soon the Christmas party was back in full swing. This time, Shrek even got to tell his own version of The Night Before Christmas.

And it was perfect!

## The Night Before Christmas

(Shrek Style)

'Twas the night before **Christmas**
and not a **swamp rat** did creep,
as mother and babe
played kazoo in their sleep.

Now, the sight of the house
would make any **ogre** droop,
'twas as sickeningly sweet as
**unicorn poop.**

Yet who was arriving
to help this lost cause?
The **foul,** the **vile,** and handsome
(heh-heh) **Ogre Claus!**

He looked all around
and scratched at his beard,
and said, **"This place is worse**
than I thought, uh, feared."

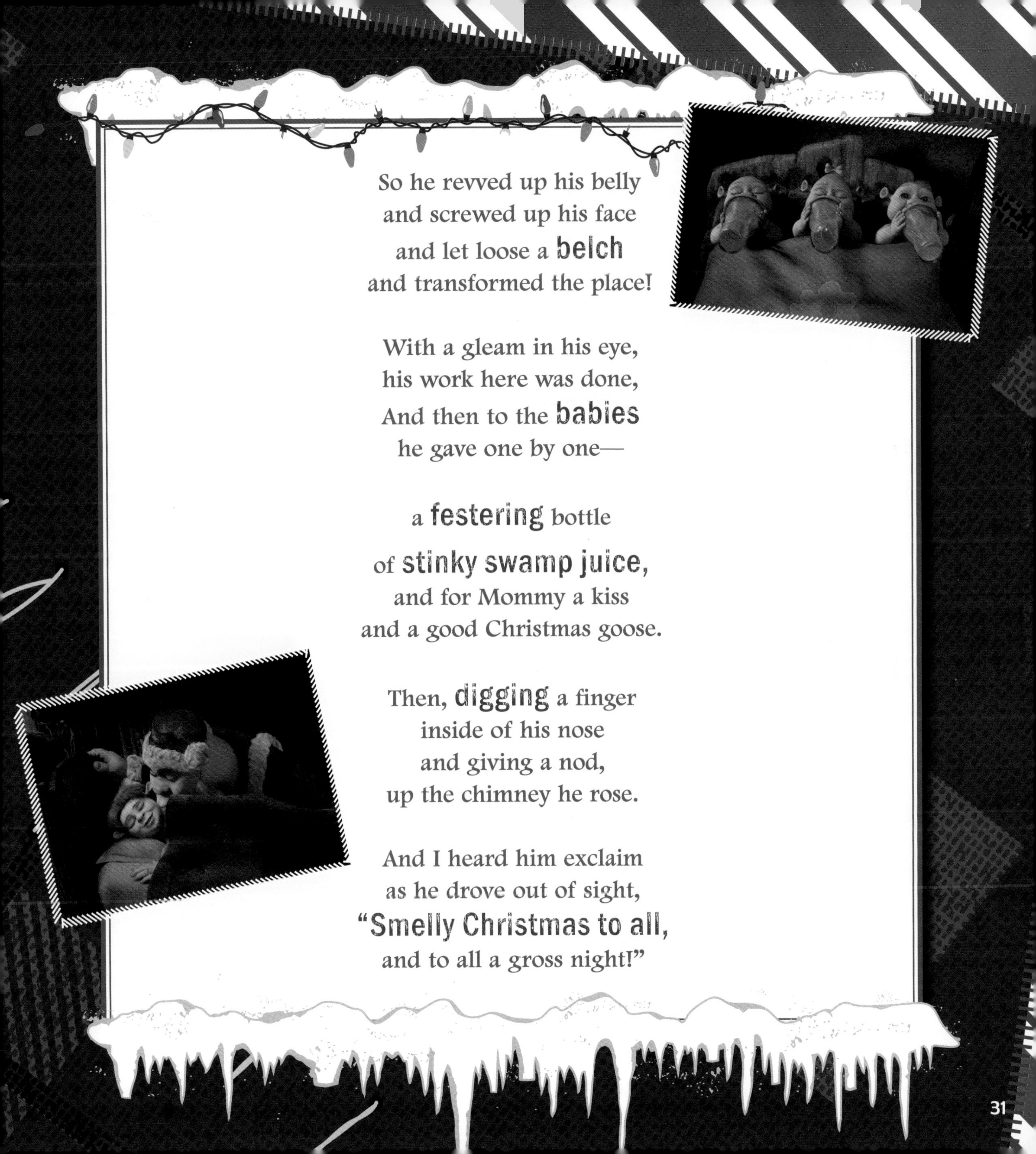

So he revved up his belly
and screwed up his face
and let loose a **belch**
and transformed the place!

With a gleam in his eye,
his work here was done,
And then to the **babies**
he gave one by one—

a **festering** bottle
of **stinky swamp juice**,
and for Mommy a kiss
and a good Christmas goose.

Then, **digging** a finger
inside of his nose
and giving a nod,
up the chimney he rose.

And I heard him exclaim
as he drove out of sight,
**"Smelly Christmas to all,**
and to all a gross night!"

I, for one, appreciate the finer
holiday decorating arts...
maybe just not on me.

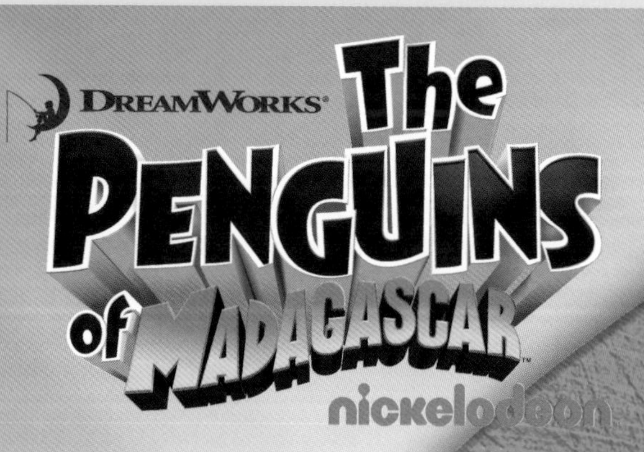


# A CHRISTMAS CAPER

TO:
FROM:

Christmas Eve had finally arrived! Throughout Central Park Zoo, festivities were in full swing among the animals. Private wanted to see how everyone was celebrating. So from the cold comfort of Penguin Headquarters, he peered through his periscope and scanned each enclosure.

The camels were dancing around their menorah.

The elephants were smooching under the mistletoe.

Alex, Marty, and Gloria were stringing bright lights around Melman's long neck.

And Mason and Phil were building—but mostly toppling—their precarious homemade Christmas tree.

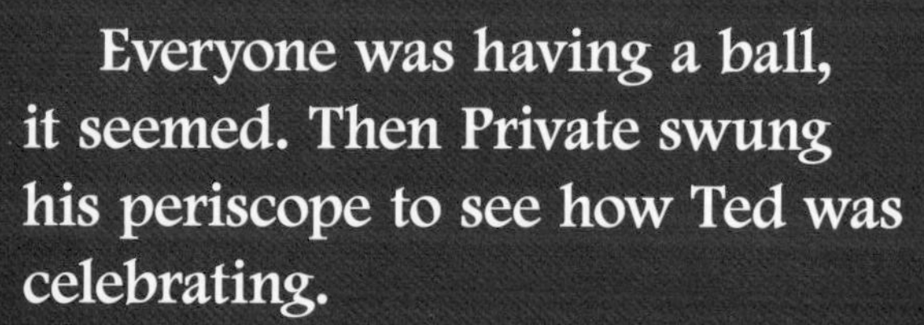

Everyone was having a ball, it seemed. Then Private swung his periscope to see how Ted was celebrating.

Only he wasn't.

The lonely polar bear lay alone in the dark. No lights. No music. No presents. No companions. No fun.

"He looks so sad," said Private. "Skipper, can we bring him a present to cheer him up?"

"Kowalski, are we equipped for such a mission?" ordered Skipper.

"Negative, Skipper," replied Kowalski. "There are four gifts and four of us, sir."

"We could go and get him something," the littlest penguin suggested hopefully.

"Sorry, Private, no can do," Skipper said definitively. "We've got eggnog at 21:00 hours and writing our names in the snow at 21:05."

Private was disheartened. He couldn't bear to see someone sad and alone on Christmas, especially with all the fun going on right in front of him.

"All right, boys, stand by for eggnog," said Skipper. "That's an order."

"Aye, aye, Skipper," said Kowalski.

"Eggnog! Eggnog! Eggnog!" added Rico.

While his merry mates were fully engaged in the spirit of Christmas, the brave young penguin took matters into his own flippers.

He slipped out of the zoo and waddled down the bustling streets of Manhattan on a lone mission to find a gift for poor, lonely Ted.

"Oh, that's perfect!" exclaimed Private when he spied a sidewalk cart full of small lighted Christmas trees. "Just the thing for a sad polar bear."

The sight of those trees made Private so happy he waddled, hopped, scaled, and shimmied his way onto the cart for a closer look at the goods.

Back at the zoo, the other penguins continued their merriment. Suddenly, Skipper's honed military senses kicked in.

"Hold on a second. Something's missing," he stated.

Kowalski surveyed the table. "Cranberries, check. Eggnog, check."

"Give me a head count, Kowalski," Skipper ordered.

"We have three heads, sir." That was it! They were missing a head . . . and the penguin it was attached to.

"Where's the private?" Skipper asked.

Kowalski pointed to Private's picture on the back of a milk carton. "Unknown, sir. It would appear that he's missing."

"Missing? Hoover Dam!" Skipper blurted.

Then he noticed Private had gone to bed. But when he removed the blanket, under the covers was a bowling pin.

Skipper looked sternly at the pin. "I'll deal with you later."

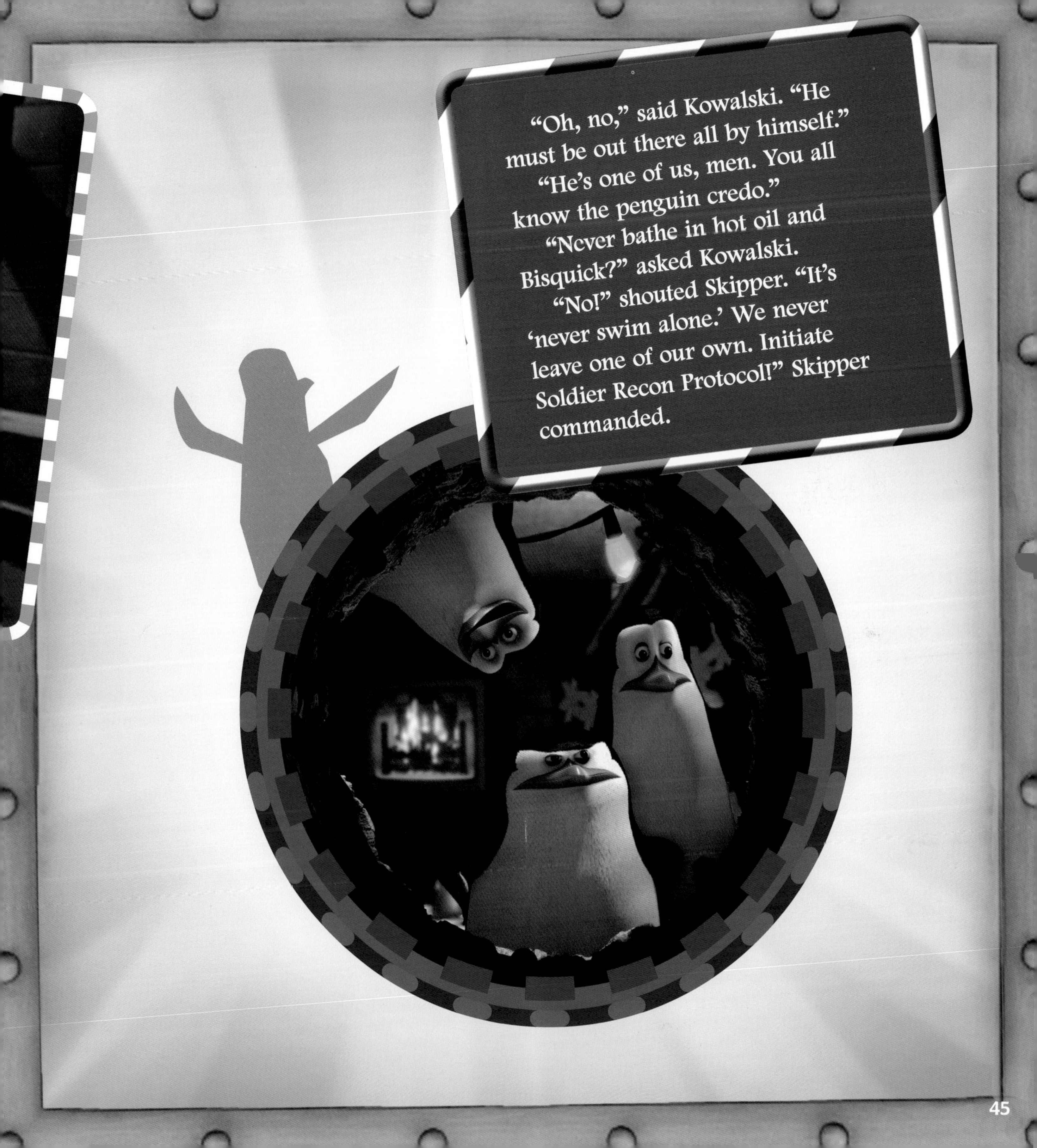

"Oh, no," said Kowalski. "He must be out there all by himself."

"He's one of us, men. You all know the penguin credo."

"Never bathe in hot oil and Bisquick?" asked Kowalski.

"No!" shouted Skipper. "It's 'never swim alone.' We never leave one of our own. Initiate Soldier Recon Protocol!" Skipper commanded.

Following Private's escape route, Skipper led his trusty soldiers on a super secret mission. Keeping a low profile, the trio sneaked through the sewer then up a manhole cover.

"Now that's using your heads, boys," said Skipper proudly.

They carefully surveyed the surroundings before stealthily emerging onto the snowy street.

The penguins investigated clues to Private's whereabouts.

"Kowalski, analysis," ordered Skipper.

Always equipped, Kowalski employed his high-tech night vision scope to scan the surroundings.

"Private located, sir."

"Good work, soldier," said Skipper. Before he could deploy the next tactic, however, Kowalski spotted something else in his scope.

"We may have a problem." Mean old Nana was heading straight for the sidewalk cart...and Private!

"Where's the gosh darn squeaker on this thing?" demanded Nana tugging, pulling, and clenching Private, mistaking him for a dog toy. When Private finally squeaked from being thoroughly squeezed, Nana bellowed, "I'll take this one!"

Before the penguins reached the cart, Nana jumped in a taxi with Private.

"Grand Coulee Dam! Private's been captured!" shouted Skipper. "Not on my watch, blue hair."

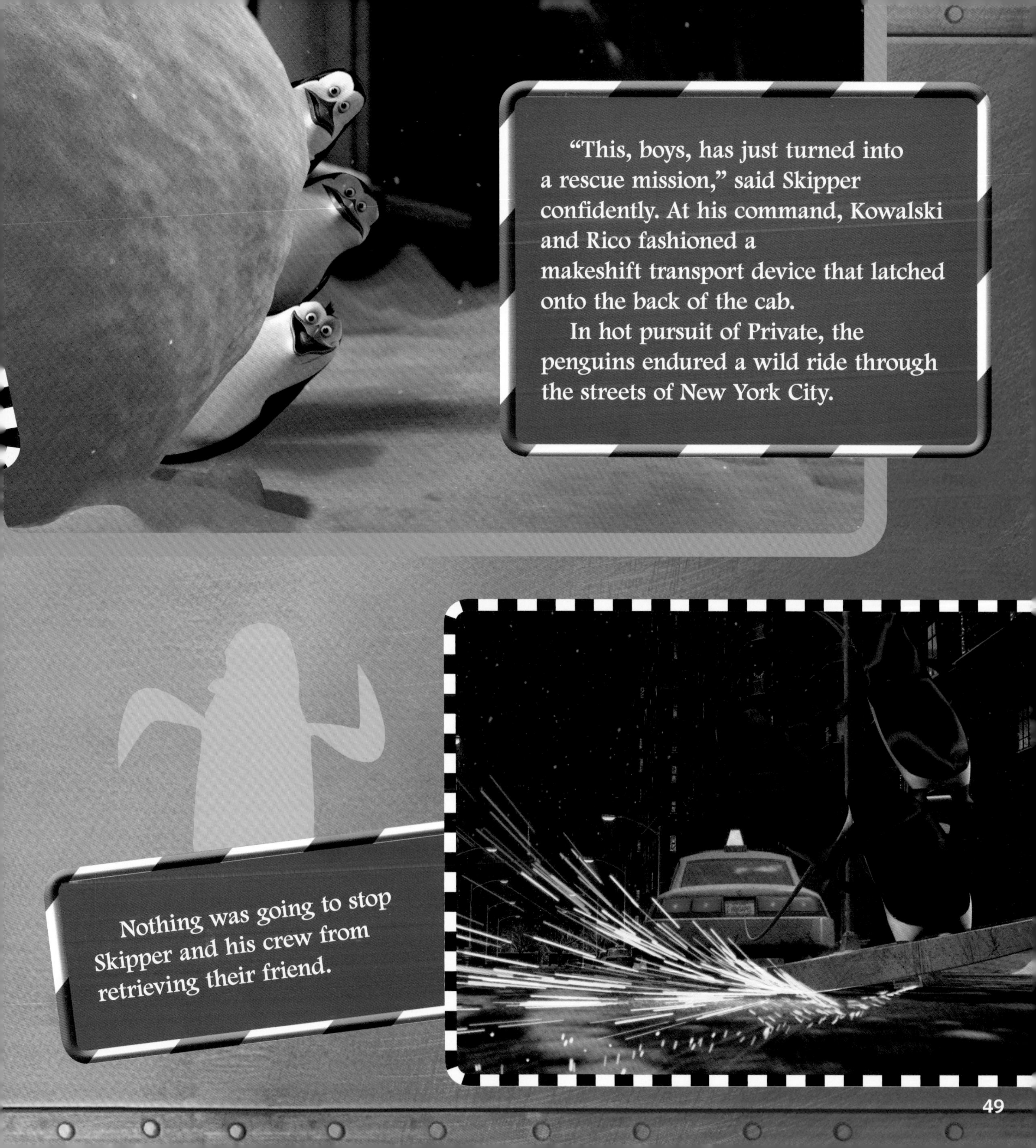

"This, boys, has just turned into a rescue mission," said Skipper confidently. At his command, Kowalski and Rico fashioned a makeshift transport device that latched onto the back of the cab.

In hot pursuit of Private, the penguins endured a wild ride through the streets of New York City.

Nothing was going to stop Skipper and his crew from retrieving their friend.

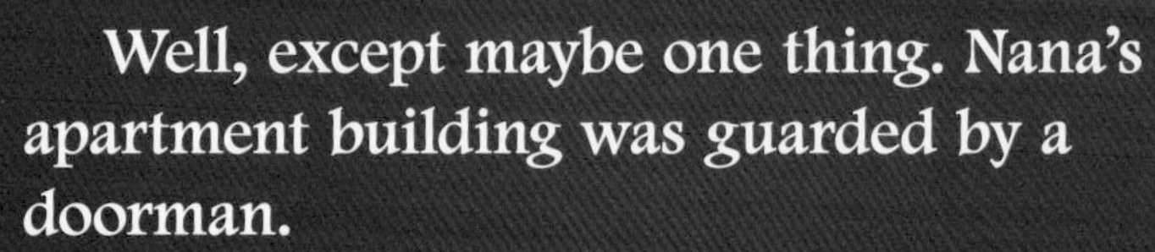

Well, except maybe one thing. Nana's apartment building was guarded by a doorman.

"Skipper, how are we going to get inside?" asked Kowalski.

"Kaboom! Kaboom!" suggested Rico, coughing up a stick of dynamite and a lighted match.

"I've got a better idea," said Skipper, dousing the flame with his flipper. "Follow me, boys."

Employing tactical measures, the resourceful trio went incognito as a snowman to gain entry.

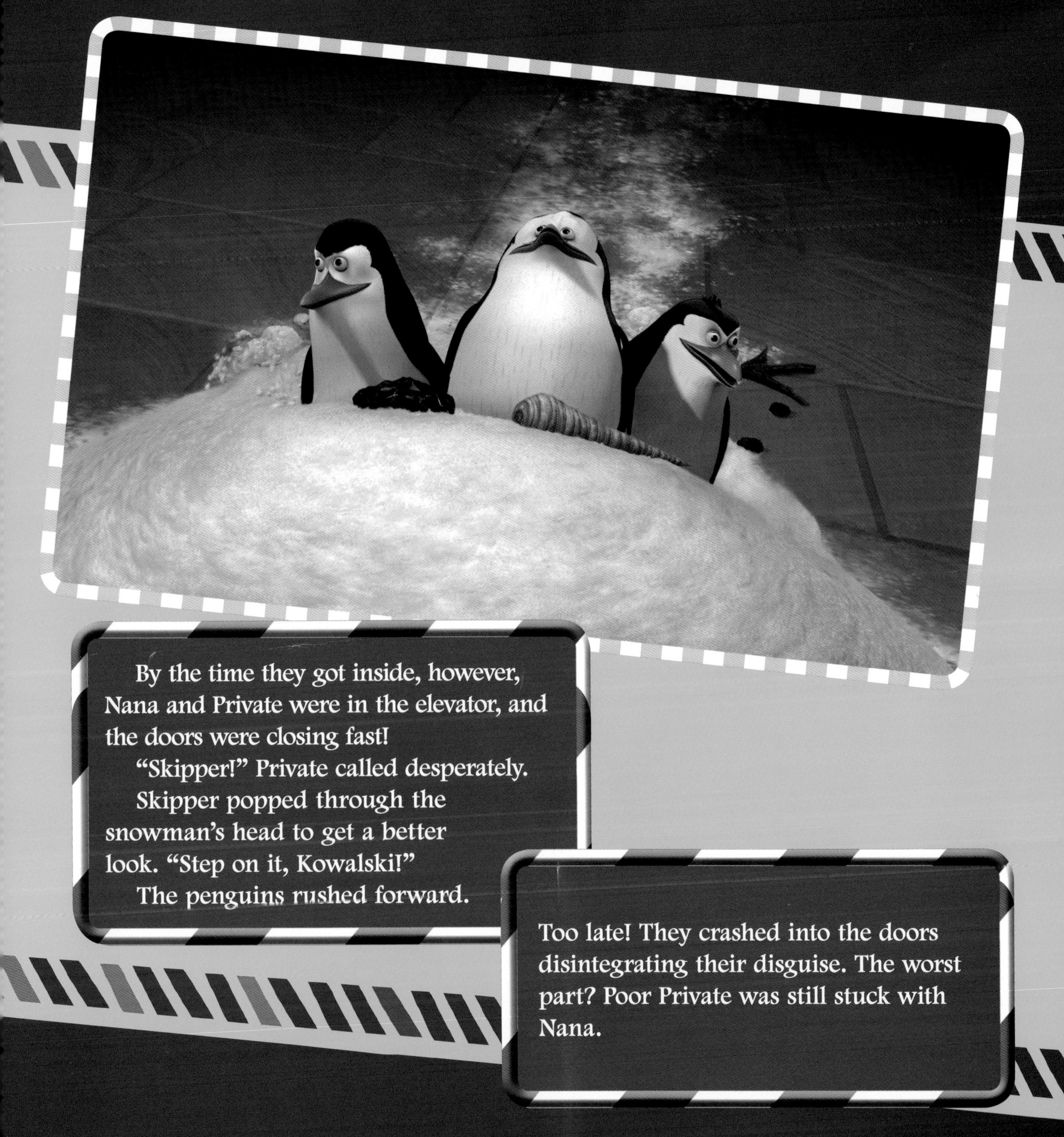

By the time they got inside, however, Nana and Private were in the elevator, and the doors were closing fast!

"Skipper!" Private called desperately.

Skipper popped through the snowman's head to get a better look. "Step on it, Kowalski!"

The penguins rushed forward.

Too late! They crashed into the doors disintegrating their disguise. The worst part? Poor Private was still stuck with Nana.

Wouldn't you know, the elevator stopped on the top floor! Skipper spied a mail chute and got an idea.

"What comes down must go up," he reasoned. "Commence Operation Special Delivery." Disguised as parcels, they loaded themselves into the chute and were rocketed up.

Standing outside Nana's front door, the penguins considered their situation. "Failure is not an option, boys," said Skipper.

Meanwhile, inside Nana's apartment things were getting worse for Private.

As if pulling, tugging, and squeezing weren't enough, Nana wrapped Private in ribbon and stuffed him into a Christmas stocking for her dog.

"Now, Mr. Chew, you have to wait until morning to open your present," Nana cooed as Mr. Chew wagged his tail.

Talking to her beloved pooch, it seemed, was the only time Nana suspended her gruff tone.

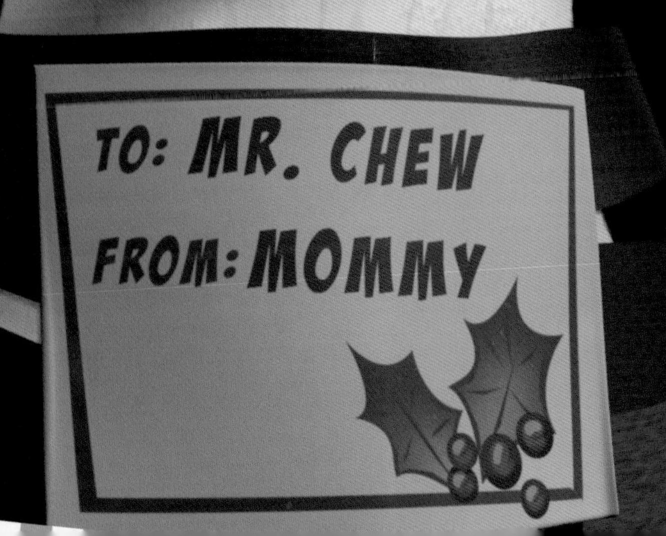

Mr. Chew may have been small, but he had a BIG attitude. When it came to his toys, he meant business. When Nana left to watch the football game, in a flash, Mr. Chew transformed from small and sweet to fierce and ferocious. Growling and baring his teeth, he ripped a stuffed toy of Alex the Lion in two! Private shook with fear.

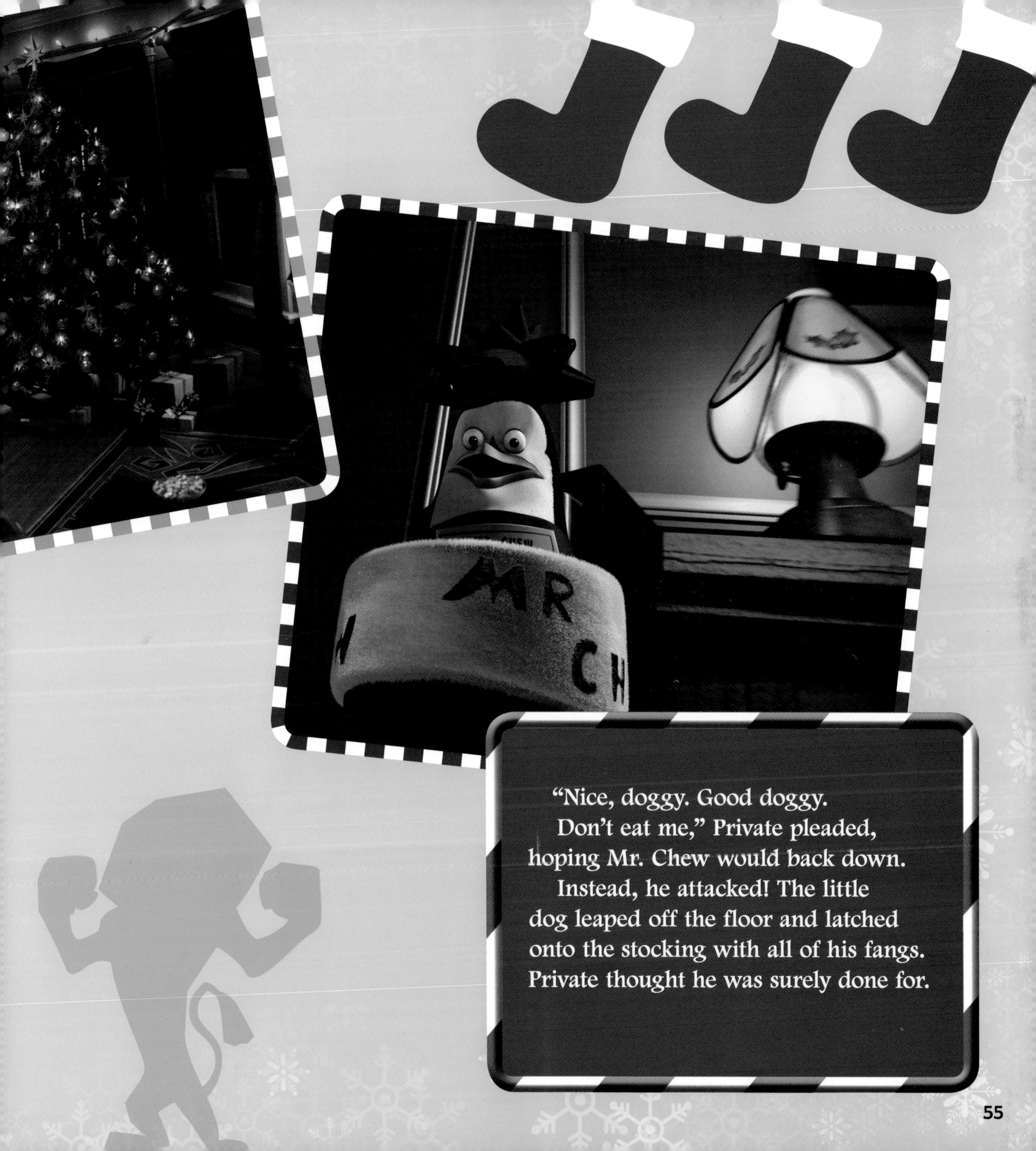

"Nice, doggy. Good doggy. Don't eat me," Private pleaded, hoping Mr. Chew would back down.

Instead, he attacked! The little dog leaped off the floor and latched onto the stocking with all of his fangs. Private thought he was surely done for.

Suddenly, Private's three penguin pals crashed through Nana's window!

"Santa Claus has come to town," said Skipper.

Just then, Mr. Chew pulled down on the stocking. When he let go to chase the other penguins, the stocking flung back up and sent Private soaring across the room. He landed atop the Christmas tree.

"Kowalski. Secure Private," Skipper ordered.

"I'll need cover fire," requested Kowalski before stealthily scaling the Christmas tree toward Private.

Rico jumped into action, swallowing a whole bowl of peppermint candies. Then, Skipper operated Rico like a rapid-fire machine gun, spraying candy at Mr. Chew to divert him from the tree.

"Kowalski. Status!"

"Almost there, Skipper," he said.

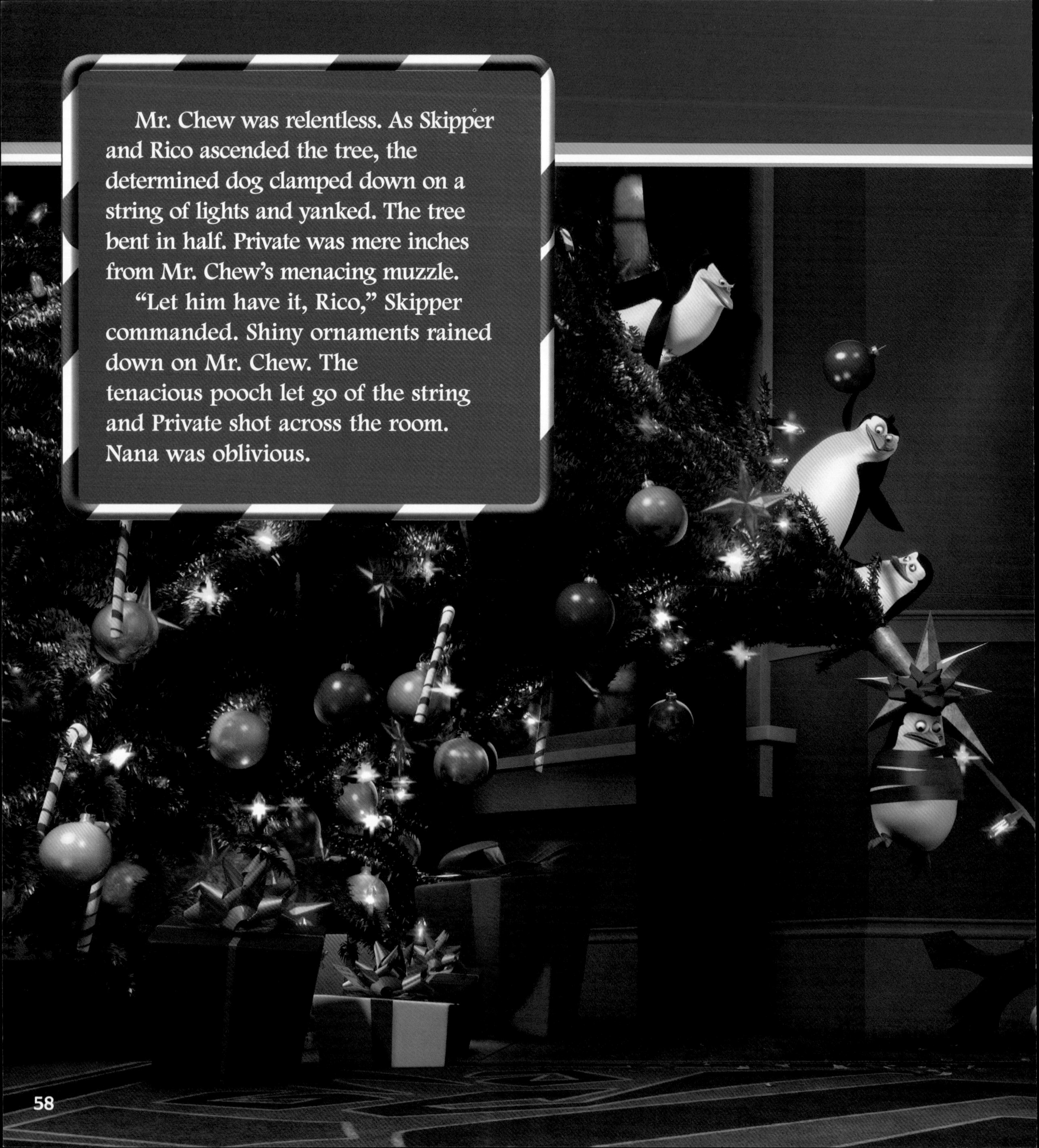

Mr. Chew was relentless. As Skipper and Rico ascended the tree, the determined dog clamped down on a string of lights and yanked. The tree bent in half. Private was mere inches from Mr. Chew's menacing muzzle.

"Let him have it, Rico," Skipper commanded. Shiny ornaments rained down on Mr. Chew. The tenacious pooch let go of the string and Private shot across the room. Nana was oblivious.

Private landed in a cooked turkey, and Mr. Chew was on him again.

"Holy butterball!" cried Skipper. The penguins needed a new plan…and fast. "Kowalski, give me options."

The shrewd soldier quickly drew up a sound strategy to end the battle once and for all.

"*Excelente,*" said Skipper. "Engage Operation Stocking Stuffer."

With a single sticky candy cane, a strand of red ribbon, and a little ingenuity, the penguins gave Mr. Chew a taste of his own medicine and stuffed him in a stocking.

"I think our work here is done," Skipper said.

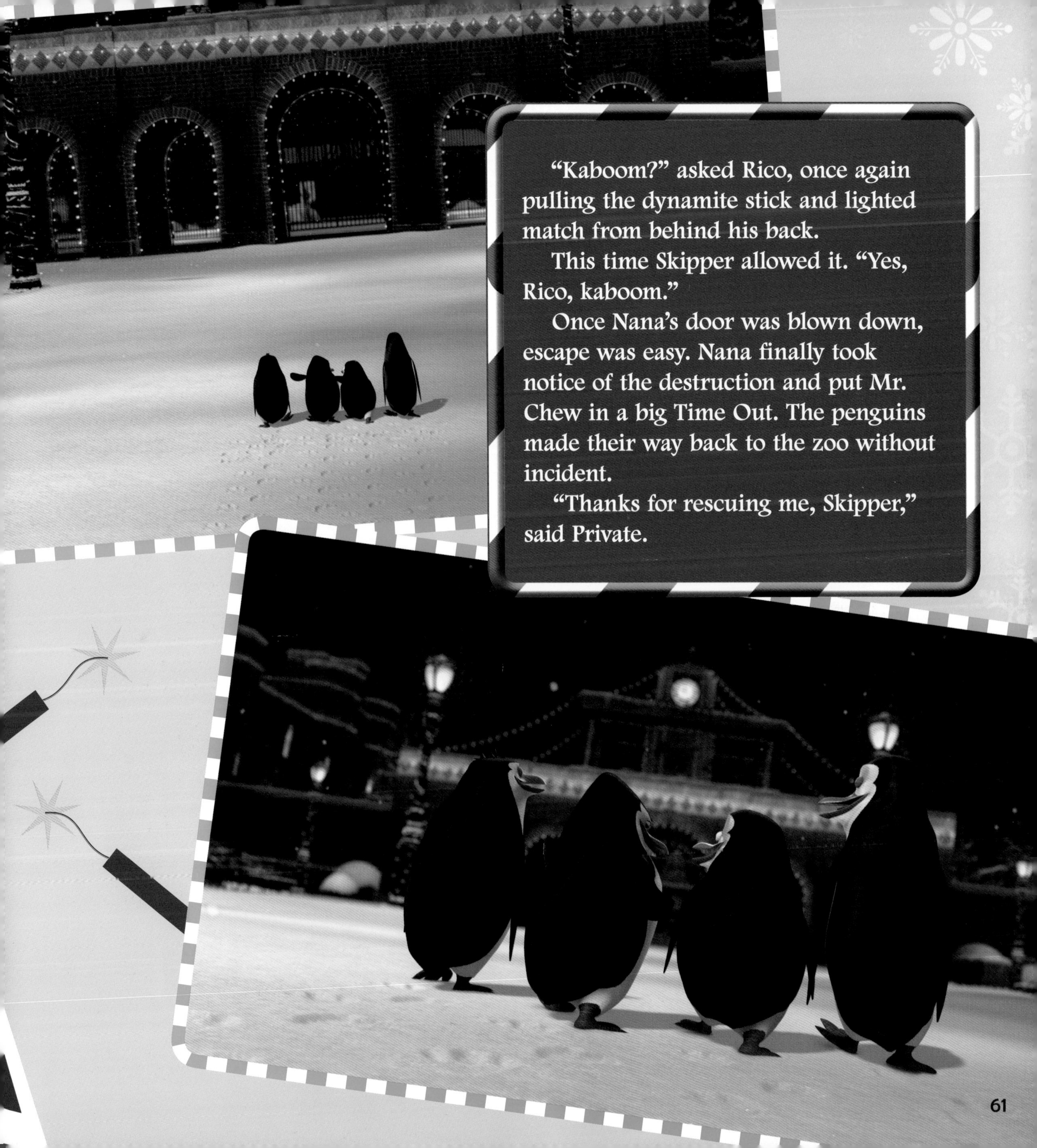

"Kaboom?" asked Rico, once again pulling the dynamite stick and lighted match from behind his back.

This time Skipper allowed it. "Yes, Rico, kaboom."

Once Nana's door was blown down, escape was easy. Nana finally took notice of the destruction and put Mr. Chew in a big Time Out. The penguins made their way back to the zoo without incident.

"Thanks for rescuing me, Skipper," said Private.

Skipper put his arm around Private. "It's the least we could do. You remember the penguin credo."

Private looked confused. "What does deep-frying in Bisquick have to do with any of this?"

Skipper was exasperated. "Not that credo. The *other* one. 'Never swim alone.'"

Remembering Ted, Private's beak fell to his chest. "He's all alone on Christmas with no one to swim with."

"It's not too late, Private," said Skipper. "I've got a new plan to fit him in."

Back at Headquarters, the penguins invited Ted over to celebrate together. Ted was so happy he snuggled all of the penguins in his arm at once.

"You guys. Seriously, this is the best Christmas I've ever had."

"Well, there it is then," said Skipper. "Merry Christmas for everyone."

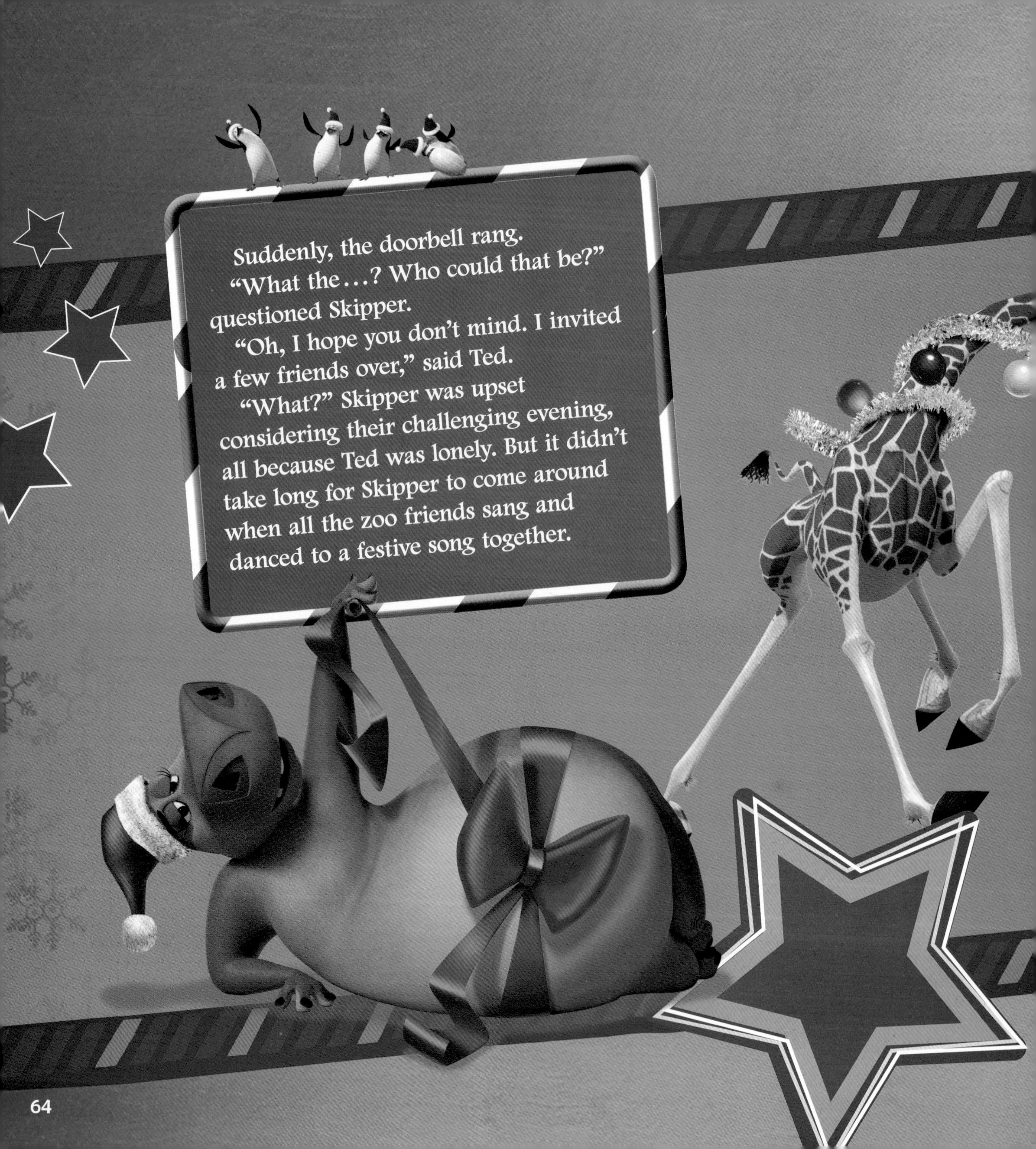

Suddenly, the doorbell rang.

"What the…? Who could that be?" questioned Skipper.

"Oh, I hope you don't mind. I invited a few friends over," said Ted.

"What?" Skipper was upset considering their challenging evening, all because Ted was lonely. But it didn't take long for Skipper to come around when all the zoo friends sang and danced to a festive song together.

Jingle Bells, monkey smells,
Melman laid an egg.
Marty thinks that Alex stinks,
And the camels say, "Oy vey!"

And that's
what Christmas
is all about.

Step aside, Rudolph,
there's a new Christmas
hero in town...Donkey!

*My Christmas wish?*
To be a real boy!
*And that's no lie.*

DreamWorks
KUNG FU PANDA
HOLIDAY

"Steel yourself against my steel, villain," declared Po in an epic battle with... an onion. He soared through the air with his cleaver and swooped down upon the potent vegetable, splitting it clean in two. "Your reign of tears is over!"

Mr. Ping was having the famed Noodle Dream. In it, he and Po were preparing a glorious batch of noodle soup together.

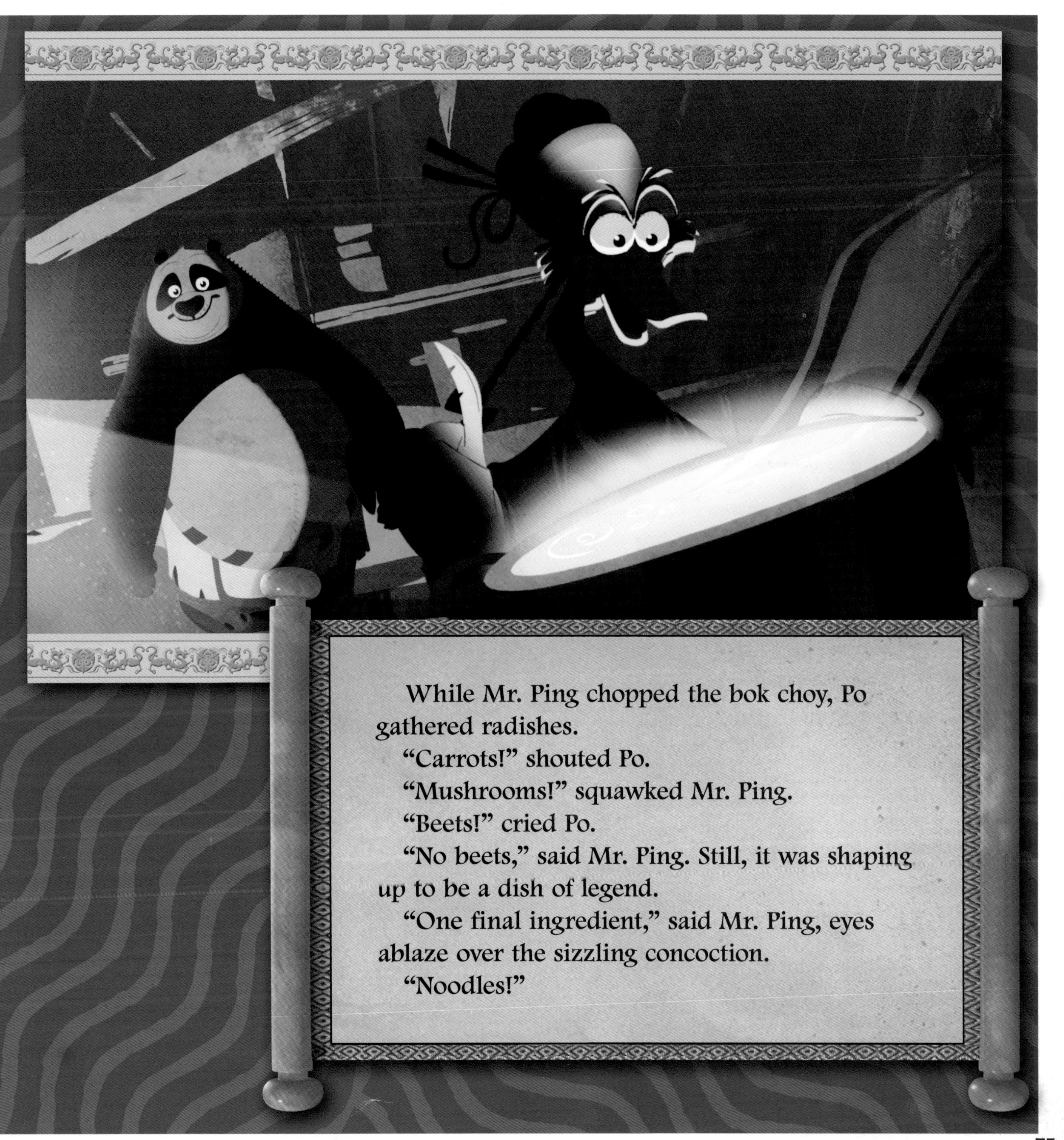

While Mr. Ping chopped the bok choy, Po gathered radishes.

"Carrots!" shouted Po.

"Mushrooms!" squawked Mr. Ping.

"Beets!" cried Po.

"No beets," said Mr. Ping. Still, it was shaping up to be a dish of legend.

"One final ingredient," said Mr. Ping, eyes ablaze over the sizzling concoction.

"Noodles!"

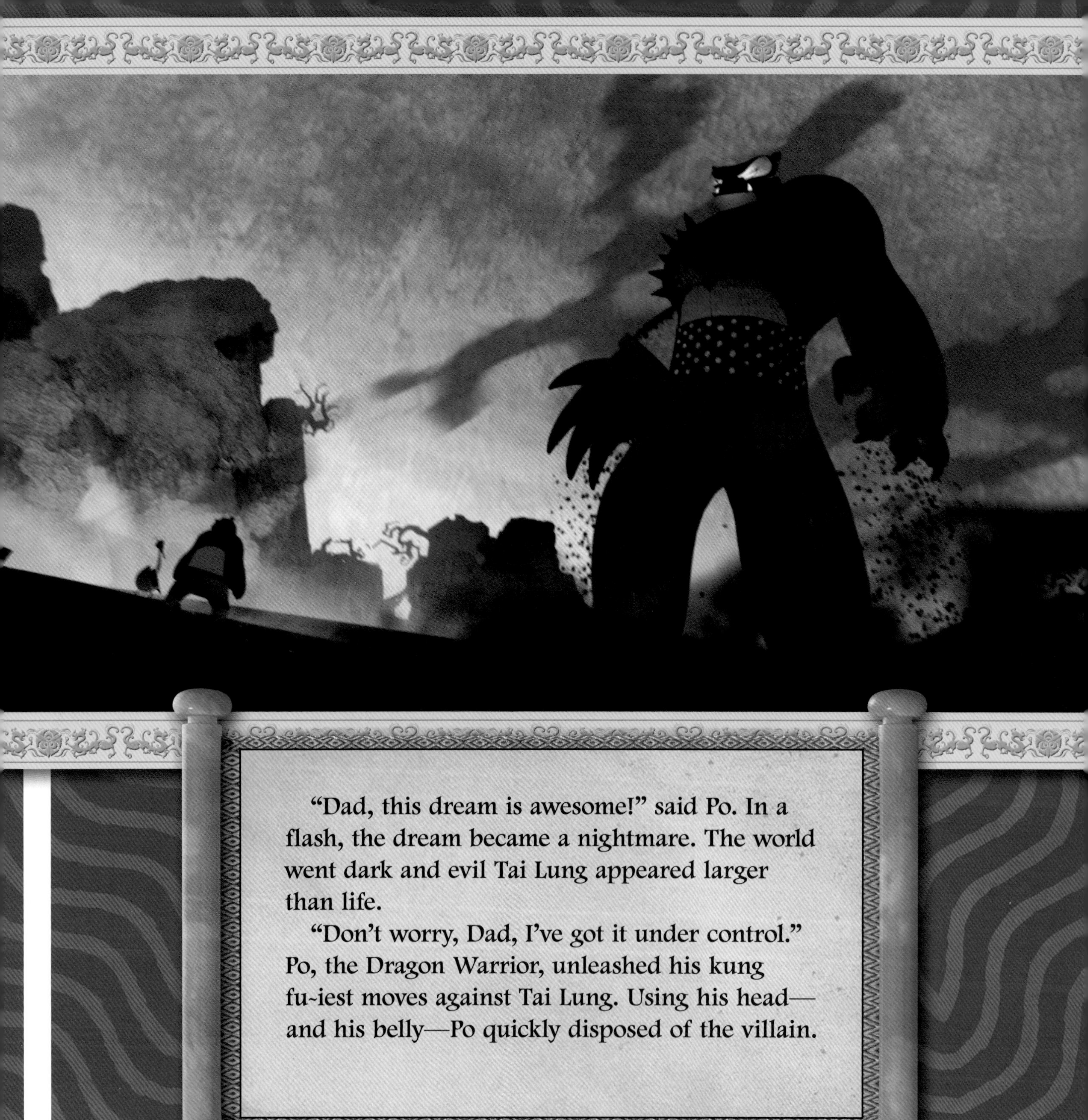

"Dad, this dream is awesome!" said Po. In a flash, the dream became a nightmare. The world went dark and evil Tai Lung appeared larger than life.

"Don't worry, Dad, I've got it under control." Po, the Dragon Warrior, unleashed his kung fu-iest moves against Tai Lung. Using his head—and his belly—Po quickly disposed of the villain.

Mr. Ping was ready to get back to work. But Po had other ideas.

"Wait! Where are you going? We're cooking together," cried Mr. Ping.

"Sorry, Dad. Evil doesn't take a holiday. And neither do I. Goodbye, Dad." With that Po left his father alone in the twisted dream, screaming after him.

Mr. Ping awoke, still yawping. Thinking his father was under attack, Po crashed through his bedroom door.

"Where'd they go? What'd they look like?" Po demanded, ready to fight.

"I was having a dream," said Mr. Ping. Then his tone turned sour. "And you left me! How could you leave me?"

Po relaxed. "Dad, it was just a dream. I'm not going anywhere."

Now that everyone was up, Po and his dad put their attention to the coming Winter Festival. They got excited just talking about the party games, the dancing, the decorations.

"Right on top," said Po, picking out an ornament. "It's the sun lantern I made when I was a cub."

Mr. Ping beamed proudly. "It was on top because I opened the box this summer just to look at it."

While Mr. Ping danced and Po ate, Master Shifu entered the kitchen. He brought news about the Winter Feast at the Jade Palace.

"With the kung fu masters from all the provinces!" Po blurted, hoping to be invited.

"You will be hosting the event," said Shifu. The giant panda nearly burst with joy.

Shifu added earnestly, "As Dragon Warrior, this is one of your most critical duties."

Po imagined the Feast to be a festive party, but Shifu explained it was just the opposite: elegant and formal.

"Awesome," Po responded. "I'm all about elegant."

Above all, noted Shifu, the Feast must be perfect. No common traditions like dancing and sun lanterns. Po was so excited Shifu had called upon him that he agreed, forgetting all about the lantern his father had saved.

"Dad, isn't this great!" exclaimed Po. In his excitement, Po had seemingly dismissed his own family traditions. Just then, the Dragon Warrior was called for duty. Rogue bandits were causing havoc at the bridge.

Dashing away, Po called, "Thanks again, Master Shifu." Mr. Ping's heart sank. His nightmare of Po leaving him to cook alone had come true.

At the bridge, Po and the Furious Five battled the bandits.

"Excited about the Winter Feast?" Po eagerly asked while blocking two charging bandits with one kung fu move.

Crane masterfully tripped raiders with spread wings. "The Feast is intense."

"It's an honor to be invited," said Mantis battling a marauder 100 times his size.

When Po told them he was hosting, the Five stopped in their tracks.

Tigress spoke gently to Po. "It's just that we think you could use a little help."

"It's a dinner. Eating. How much do you have to know?" Po asked. A lot, it turned out. For starters, "There are 18 gestures you must memorize for the right hand," said Shifu to Po as the two moved through the palace. The most difficult part for Po was that no guests were allowed.

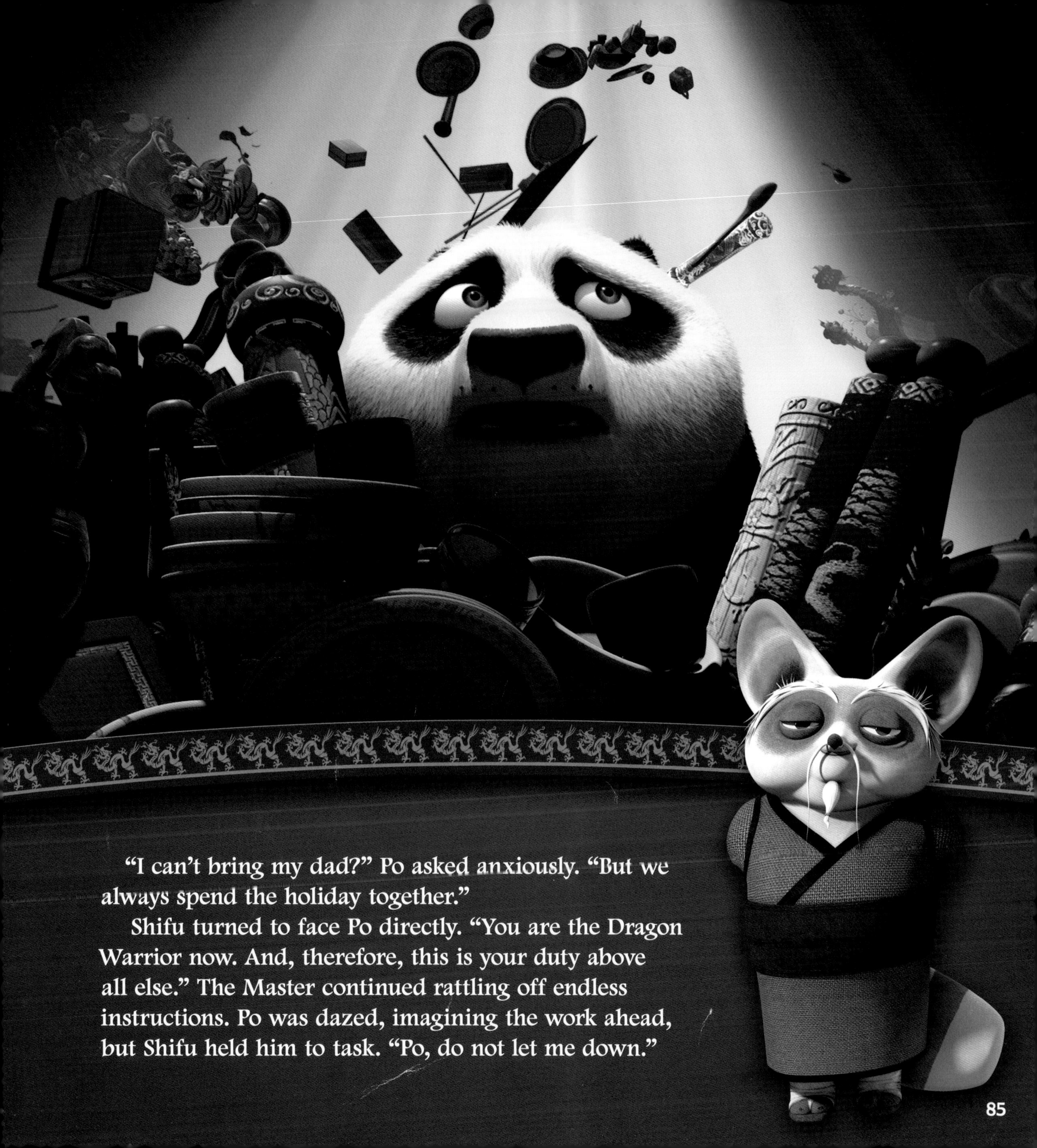

"I can't bring my dad?" Po asked anxiously. "But we always spend the holiday together."

Shifu turned to face Po directly. "You are the Dragon Warrior now. And, therefore, this is your duty above all else." The Master continued rattling off endless instructions. Po was dazed, imagining the work ahead, but Shifu held him to task. "Po, do not let me down."

Po's first duty was to hire a chef. In the courtyard, Zeng assembled a long line of culinary masters.

"Master Po, we have brought you the finest chefs in China," began Zeng. "You'll sample the dishes, then you'll make your choice." Po's mouth watered. "The chef you select will receive the Golden Ladle. Let us begin."

"Alrighty!" declared Po.

Chef Wo Hop was up first. As he began his presentation, Monkey entered the courtyard. Po waved to his friend and, in a flash, two guards whisked Wo Hop away.

"Whoa, what just happened?" asked Po.

Zeng dutifully reminded him that, as host of the festival, every gesture had meaning. Po had inadvertently performed the ancient Hun Shu Wave of Dismissal, causing Wo Hop great dishonor and eternal shame.

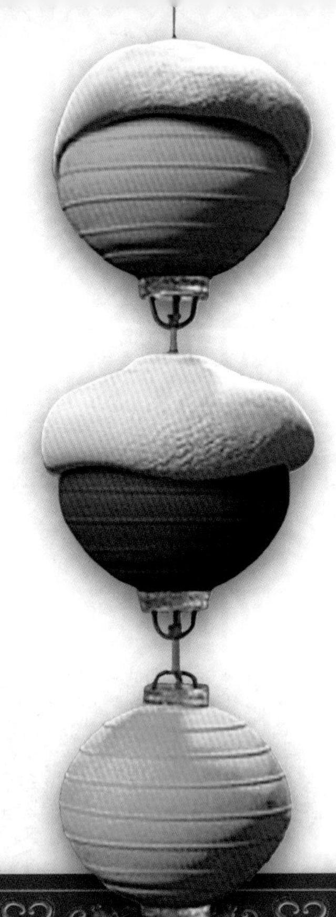

"Wow, this Feast is intense," said Po. "*And,* I can't be with my dad." Thinking about his father, Po got an idea. "That's it! I'll choose my dad as chef!"

First, Po had to properly dismiss the other chefs. He sampled a dish. "This isn't really what we're looking for," he said. He sampled another. "Nope." After the last tasting, Po grabbed the box with the Golden Ladle and dashed home.

Mr. Ping was almost in tears. "The Golden Ladle. What an extraordinary honor. When is the Feast?"

"Tomorrow," said Po.

Mr. Ping handed the ladle back to Po. "That won't work. It's the holiday. My customers are counting on me."

This put Po in a real pickle. He really wanted to be with his dad, but as the Dragon Warrior, Po had important obligations.

Since Po had no chef, he headed to the kitchen to start cooking by himself. Moments later, Wo Hop appeared.

"I am here to fight the Dragon Warrior," the bunny said. "It's the only way I can lift the veil of shame. Surely I will die, but it will restore my honor." Po felt bad about Wo Hop's predicament, but he didn't have time to fight.

Time was running out. Po had to prepare the feast, select a vocalist, have a costume fitting, carve an ice sculpture, and set the table...all by himself. It was too much!

All the while Po was struggling, Mr. Ping was also having a difficult time trying to run his restaurant alone.

"This is a total disaster," sighed Po. "Now I'm going to disappoint everyone."

Po threw up his hands. "What kind of Dragon Warrior am I if I can't even pull off a dinner?"

"I guess kung fu can't solve everything," Wo Hop said. Or could it?

Po darted off and called on the Furious Five to prepare them for what might be their greatest challenge ever.

"Bandits?" asked Monkey.

"No," said Po. "Place settings."

"Mantis, Pinwheel Attack!" ordered Po. Mantis kung fu kicked a stack of plates into precise position. The other masters employed their best moves to finish setting the table.

"Bunny, if you even want me to think about your death with honor, you'll have to help me in the kitchen." Wo Hop reluctantly agreed. Finally, the Feast was ready, except for one tiny detail.

"*Ground* jasmine?" Po screamed. "It was supposed to be *flaked!*"

"I promised Master Shifu everything would be perfect!" Po fled to the village for proper jasmine. Once there, Po fell under the spell of colorful holiday lights, hand-painted sun lanterns hanging in windows, and families gathered together. The gentle panda quietly sighed, missing his father terribly. Conflicted and heartbroken, the Dragon Warrior returned to the palace where the Winter Feast was about to begin.

At the Feast, Shifu was impressed with Po's work. "Elegant. Perfect. You've made me proud." Po was honored. But he was not happy. When Shifu urged him to recite the Creed of the Masters, Po instead recalled his fondest holiday memories.

"I wish I could stay and be a good host but I need to leave and," Po looked at Shifu, "be a good son."

Inspired by Po's holiday stories, the kung fu masters recalled memories of their own families.

"I used to love cooking with my sisters," said Viper.

Tigress grinned thinking of her favorite traditions. "The folk dances..."

"Games! The music!" said Crane. All of that festive talk upset Shifu, who was concerned only about kung fu traditions.

Back in the village, Mr. Ping was thrilled to see Po. He felt sorry for making his son feel guilty about his obligation.

"That's what the holidays are all about," smiled Po. "Now, don't we have some cookin' to do?"

With swift culinary moves rivaling any kung fu master, father and son whipped up their famous noodle soup for all the hungry villagers. Po never felt happier.

Everything was perfect. Sun lanterns were hung, including Po's. Festive music played. Villagers slurped soup. Even Po's uncle Yang, who laughs so hard he shoots noodles out of his nose, was there. To Po's surprise and delight, the Five and the other kung fu masters arrived to join the party.

"The more the merrier," said Mr. Ping.

Everyone enjoyed the festivities, except Wo Hop who still hadn't fought the Dragon Warrior. Stealthily, he stalked Po.

"Yiy-yiy-yiy-yiy!" he lunged. But the Dragon Warrior was quick. He turned, holding the Golden Ladle.

"I believe this is yours," Po said graciously.

"Oh, thank you, Dragon Warrior." Wo Hop's snarl curled to a smile. "Now I have restored my honor and the honor of my village."

Meanwhile, alone, Shifu trudged through the snow toward Mr. Ping's.

"Oh, Po, why did you ruin something that was perfect?" the kung fu master wondered aloud. But when he peeked into the restaurant, he spotted Master Rhino telling scary stories. Mantis played peek-a-boo with a giggling bunny. And Po helped his dad serve happy customers.

Shifu's eyes softened. At last, he understood. "THIS is perfect."

Po spied Shifu outside. "There's always ro
Mr. Ping's!"

Shifu didn't want to disturb Po's fa

"You're my family, too," Po gently s
conceded. "That soup does smell delic
inside, but Shifu paused.

"Po, what goes on in your head I really don't always
understand, but what goes on in your heart will never let
us down."

illagers were impressed
e such a kung fu legend at
party.

"It's good to see you, Master Shifu," said Mr. Ping excitedly, forgetting all about Po's leaving for the Winter Feast.

"And it's good to be here, Mr. Ping." Shifu said, sitting at the head of the table surrounded by Po, Mr. Ping, and his best students.

Po smiled over the crowd. He'd managed to make both his dad and Shifu proud. And from the tiniest, giggliest children to the strongest, wisest, coolest kung fu masters, everyone was enjoying the celebration together. This was the best holiday ever.

"Thanks for coming, everyone!"

T-minus 24 hours till Christmas...
Initiate Joyful Protocol
Mission
Ho-Ho-Holiday Cheer!

Christmas isn't Christmas
without schnitzel!

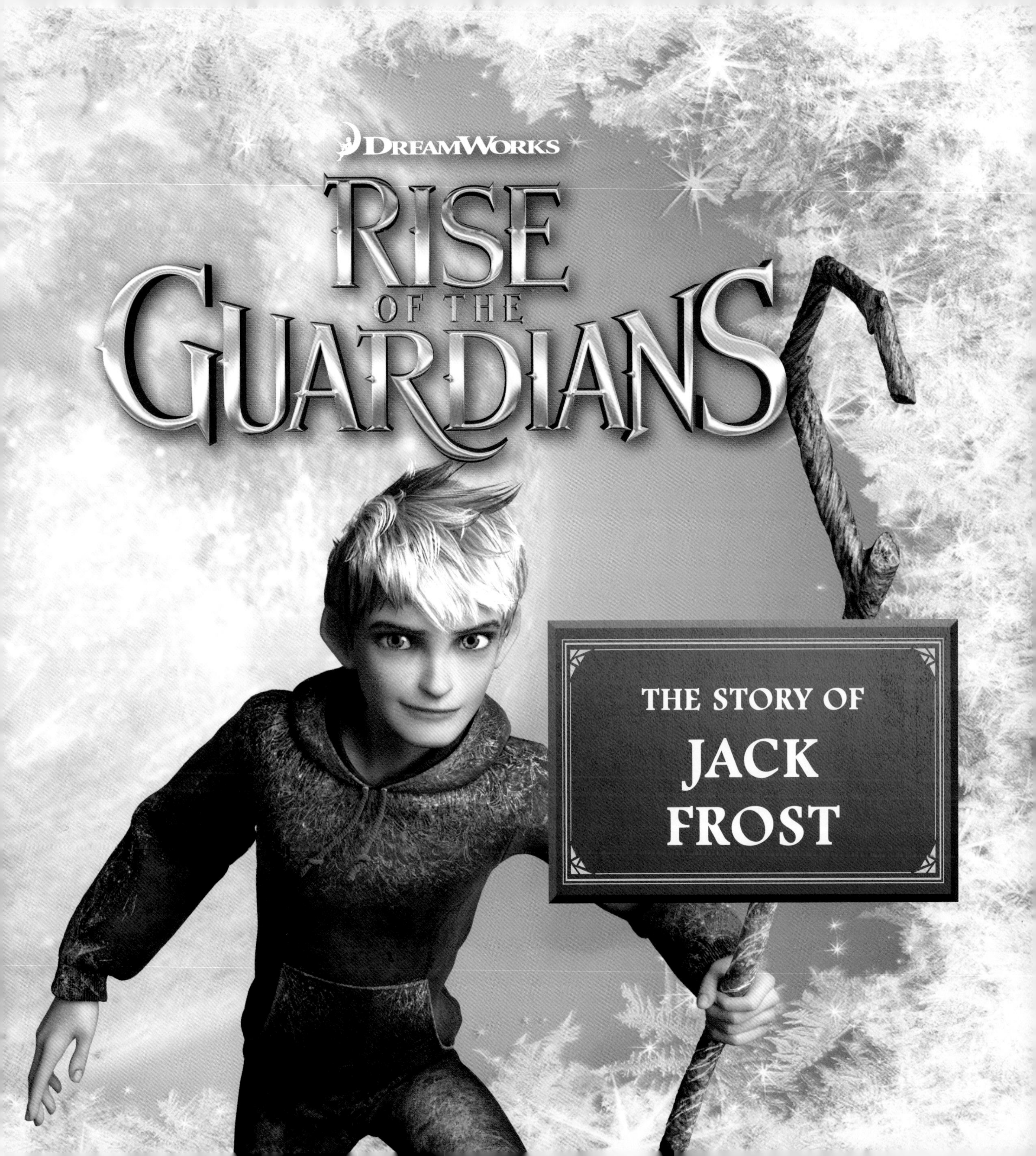
DreamWorks
RISE OF THE GUARDIANS
THE STORY OF
JACK
FROST

My name is Jack Frost. How do I know that? The Man in the Moon told me so. But that's all he ever told me.

For a long time I wondered who I was and what I was meant to do. It would take me many years to find out.
This is my story...

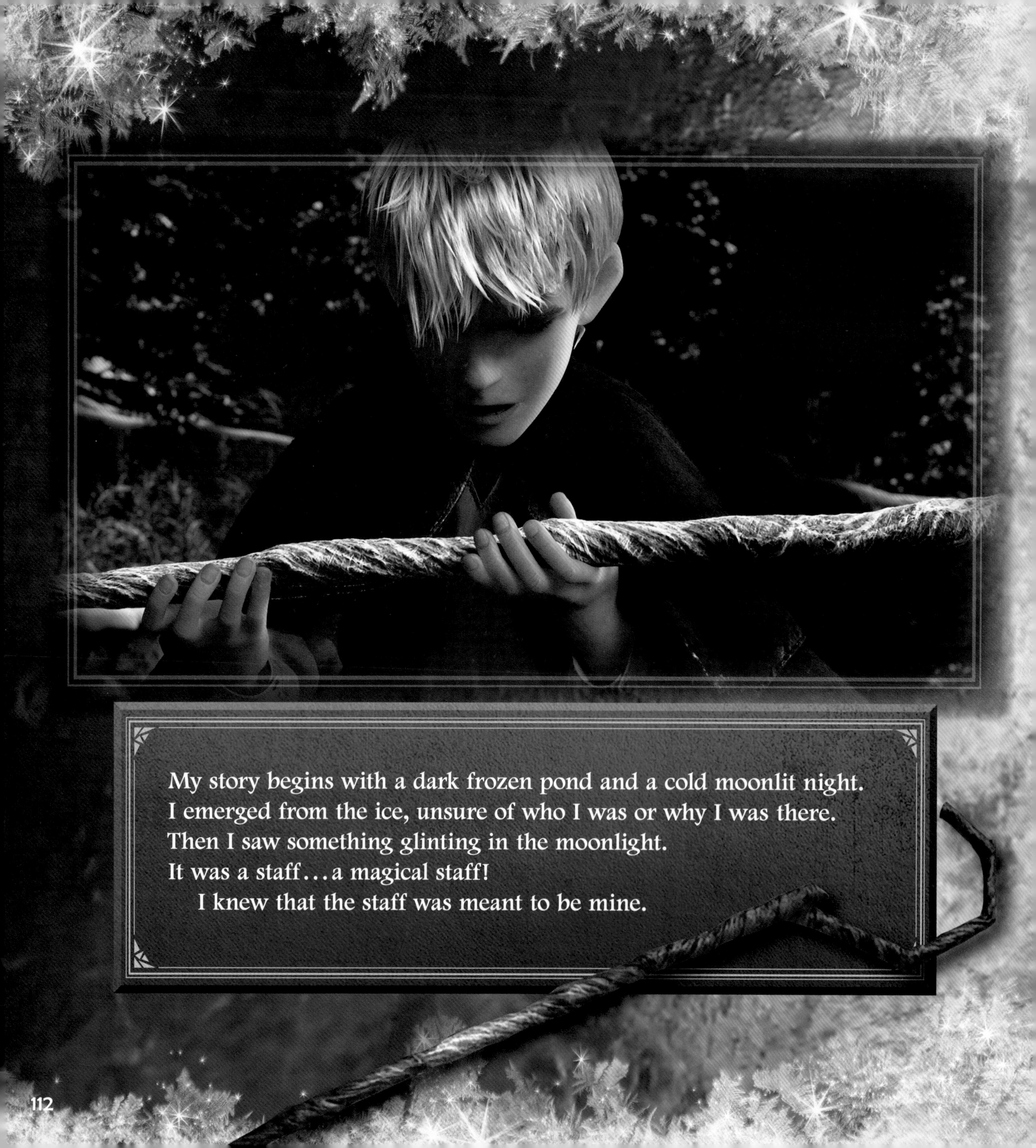

My story begins with a dark frozen pond and a cold moonlit night. I emerged from the ice, unsure of who I was or why I was there. Then I saw something glinting in the moonlight. It was a staff...a magical staff!

I knew that the staff was meant to be mine.

This staff was like a magic wand but even better! By using it, I could create ice and frost!

"How about some ice with that water, Jamie?"

I quickly discovered what an awesome power this was…and how much fun I could have with it!

"Be careful you don't slip on the iiiiice!"

Have you ever had the day off from school for a snow day? Well, that was me! I can create snow days!

Jamie and his friends needed some help starting a snowball fight. Do you know the best way to start one? It's simple, really...just throw a snowball!

If you're invisible like me, then no one can tell where it came from and voila...instant snowball fight!

The fun ended when Jamie lost his tooth. But he didn't care because he knew it meant the tooth fairy would be coming that night.

I watched and waited with Jamie for Tooth to come, but I wasn't very happy about it. You see, the tooth fairy brings joy to children, and the children believe in her. But what about me? I bring joy to them with snow days and winter fun, but no one believed in me. And because they didn't believe in me, no one could see me.

Later that night I was captured by Yetis and whisked to the North Pole! And by whisked—I mean that the Yetis shoved me in a sack, and I was tossed like a piece of luggage through a magic portal.
It wasn't exactly a pleasant trip, but I was excited to see North's workshop. I had tried to break in for years!

I couldn't believe who was waiting for me at North's palace: North, the big guy himself, Easter Bunny, Tooth Fairy, and the Sandman. Together they are known as the Guardians of Childhood.

My first words to North were, "You've gotta be kidding me!" But they weren't kidding!

Why did the Guardians drag me all the way to their big meeting at the North Pole? Well, they wanted me to join them!

They told me that the Man in the Moon had chosen me to help protect the children of the world from Pitch...whom you may know as the boogeyman.

I told them they were wrong...that I wasn't meant to be a Guardian.

"You're hard work and deadlines. I'm snowballs and fun times," I told them. In other words...thanks, but no thanks.

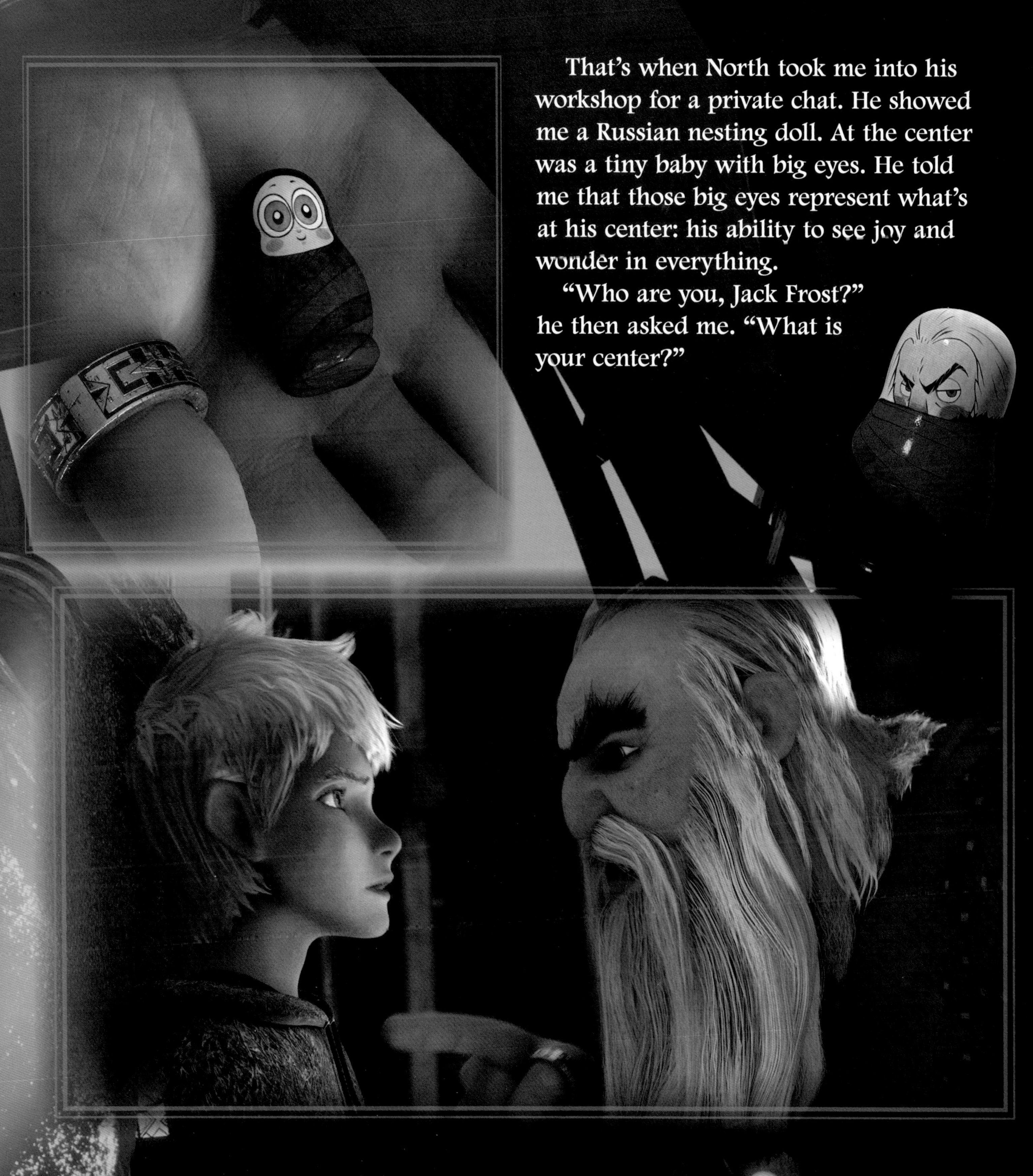

That's when North took me into his workshop for a private chat. He showed me a Russian nesting doll. At the center was a tiny baby with big eyes. He told me that those big eyes represent what's at his center: his ability to see joy and wonder in everything.

"Who are you, Jack Frost?" he then asked me. "What is your center?"

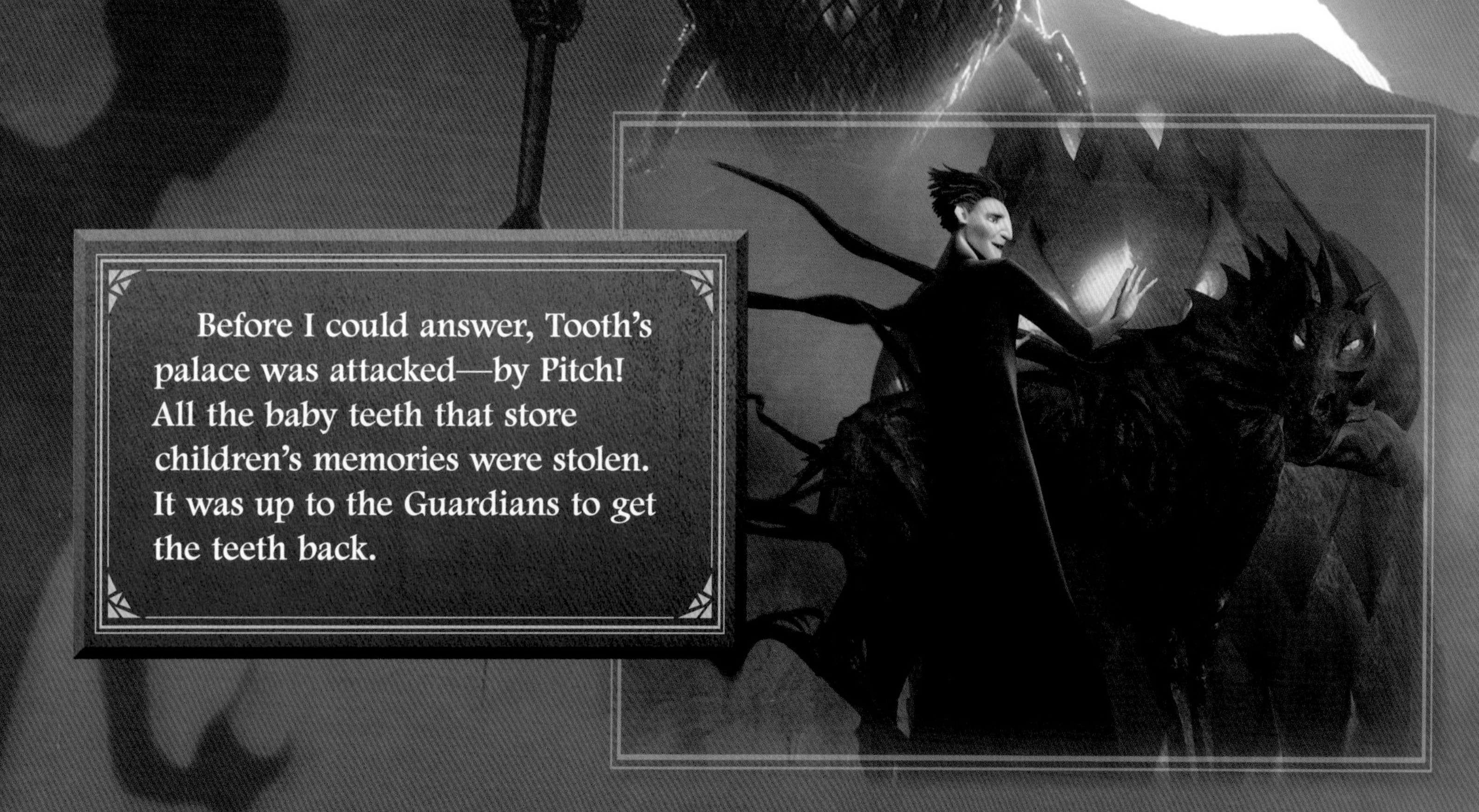

Before I could answer, Tooth's palace was attacked—by Pitch! All the baby teeth that store children's memories were stolen. It was up to the Guardians to get the teeth back.

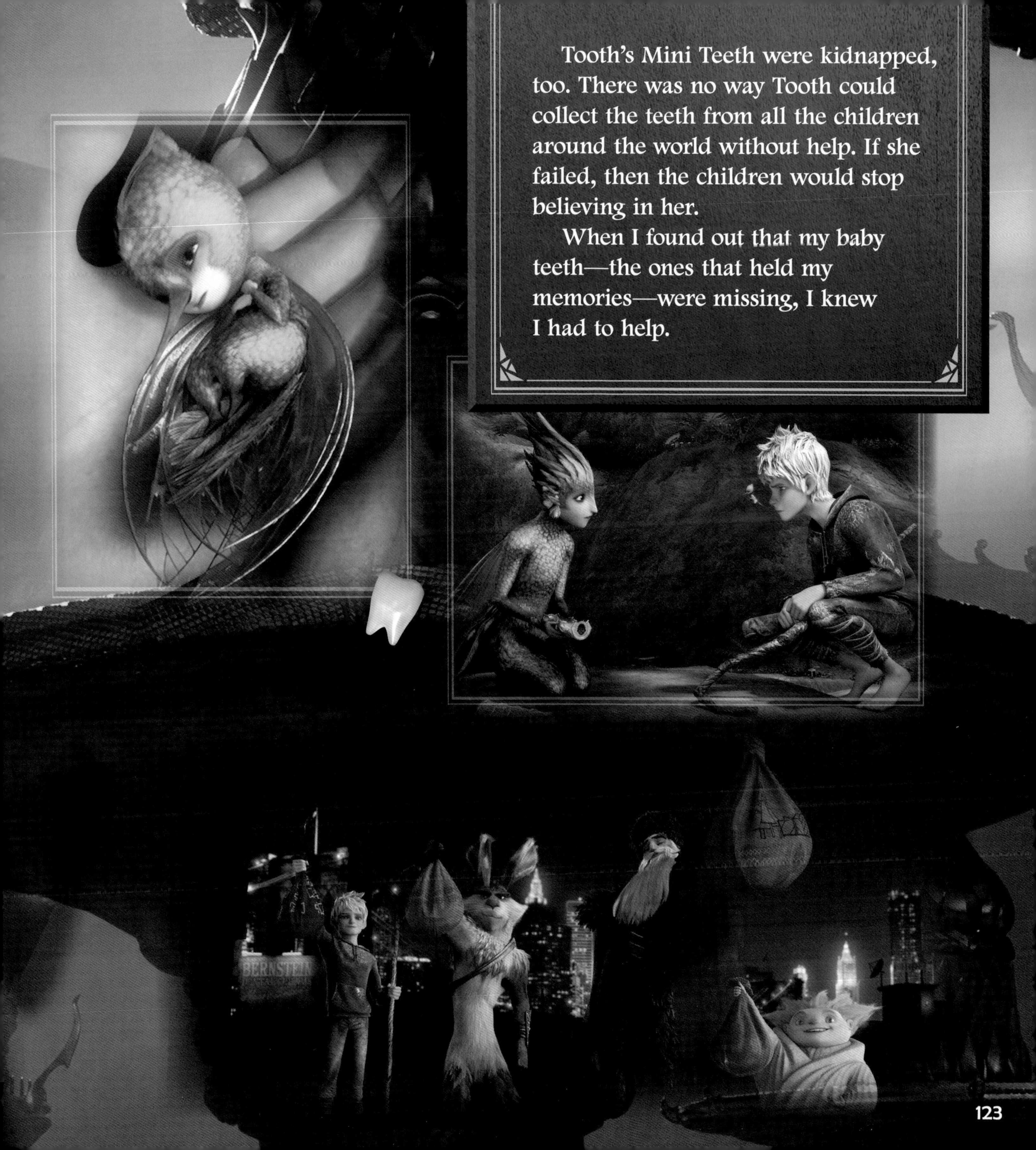

Tooth's Mini Teeth were kidnapped, too. There was no way Tooth could collect the teeth from all the children around the world without help. If she failed, then the children would stop believing in her.

When I found out that my baby teeth—the ones that held my memories—were missing, I knew I had to help.

But Pitch had only just begun. He went on to launch a full-blown attack against the Guardians. Pitch's nightmares gave terrible dreams to children, and they stopped believing in the Sandman.

Then Easter was ruined, and children stopped believing in the Easter Bunny.

And it was my fault. I let Pitch get away because he used my teeth to distract me.

I almost had him! I'd chased Pitch through his dark tunnels until I caught him. But the lure of my baby teeth—my memories—was too strong.

Ultimately, I found out who I was! I had saved my sister long ago. I was a hero! But just as I figured that out, I realized it might be too late. North was right—the Man in the Moon was never wrong. I was brave enough to be a Guardian.

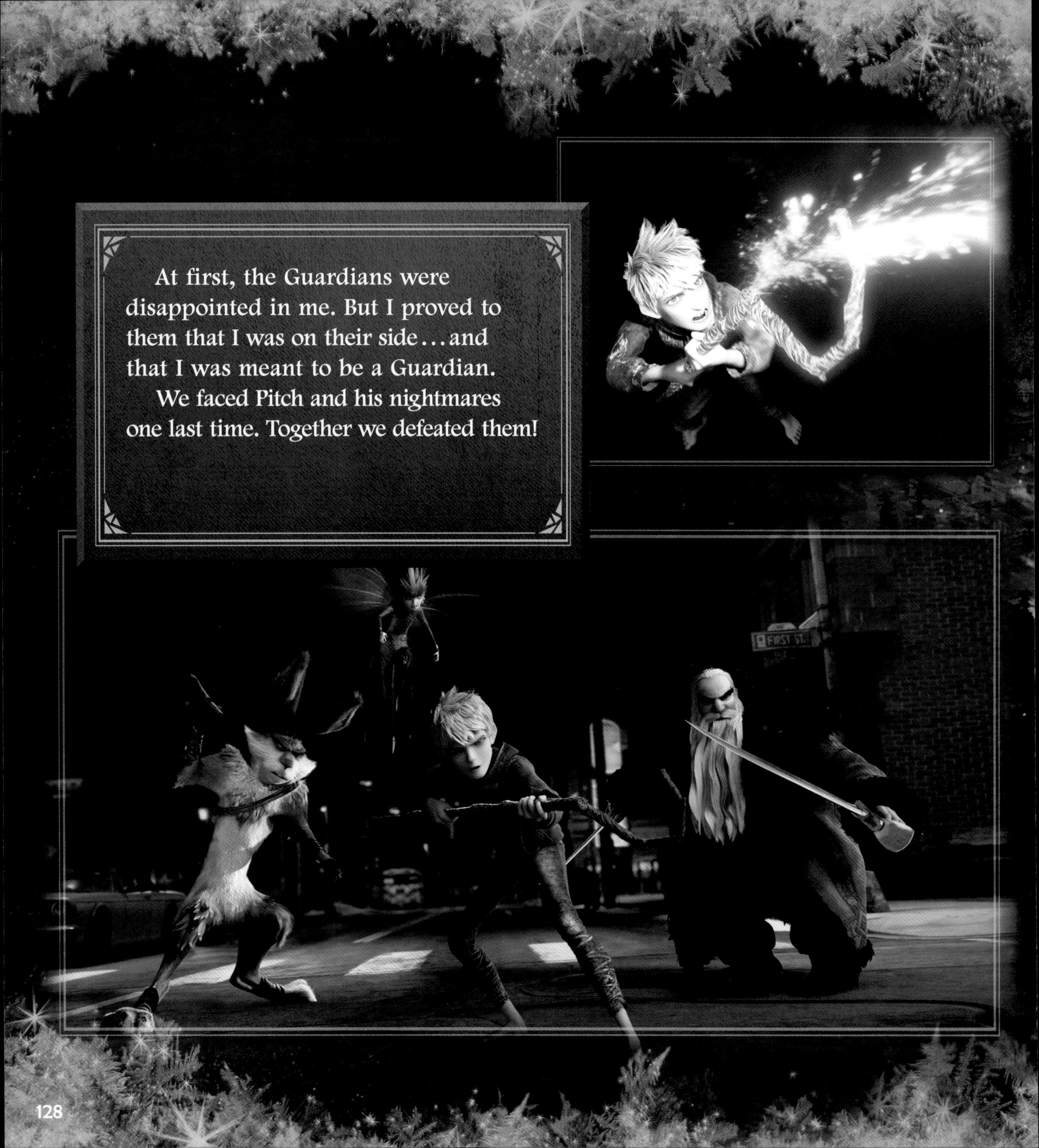


At first, the Guardians were disappointed in me. But I proved to them that I was on their side . . . and that I was meant to be a Guardian.

We faced Pitch and his nightmares one last time. Together we defeated them!

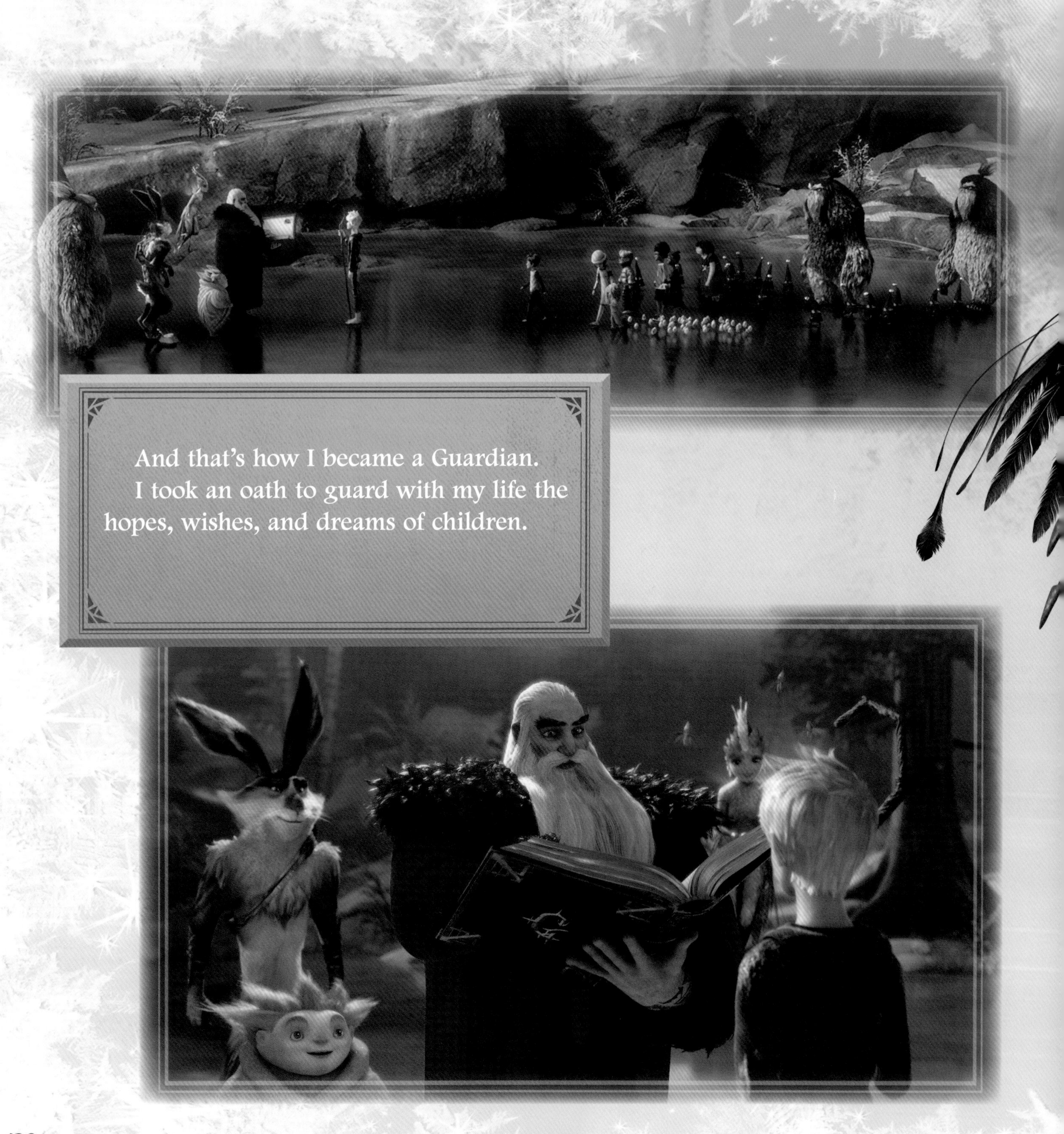

And that's how I became a Guardian.

I took an oath to guard with my life the hopes, wishes, and dreams of children.

I will always be there to guard and protect you.

And the next time you have a snow day…think of me and start an awesome snowball fight. Just remember to duck!

I've got this. Christmas toys. Christmas joys. Christmas fun for girls and boys.

Ho, ho, ho, kids!
Santa Claus here.
Looks like no one made the
naughty list this year!

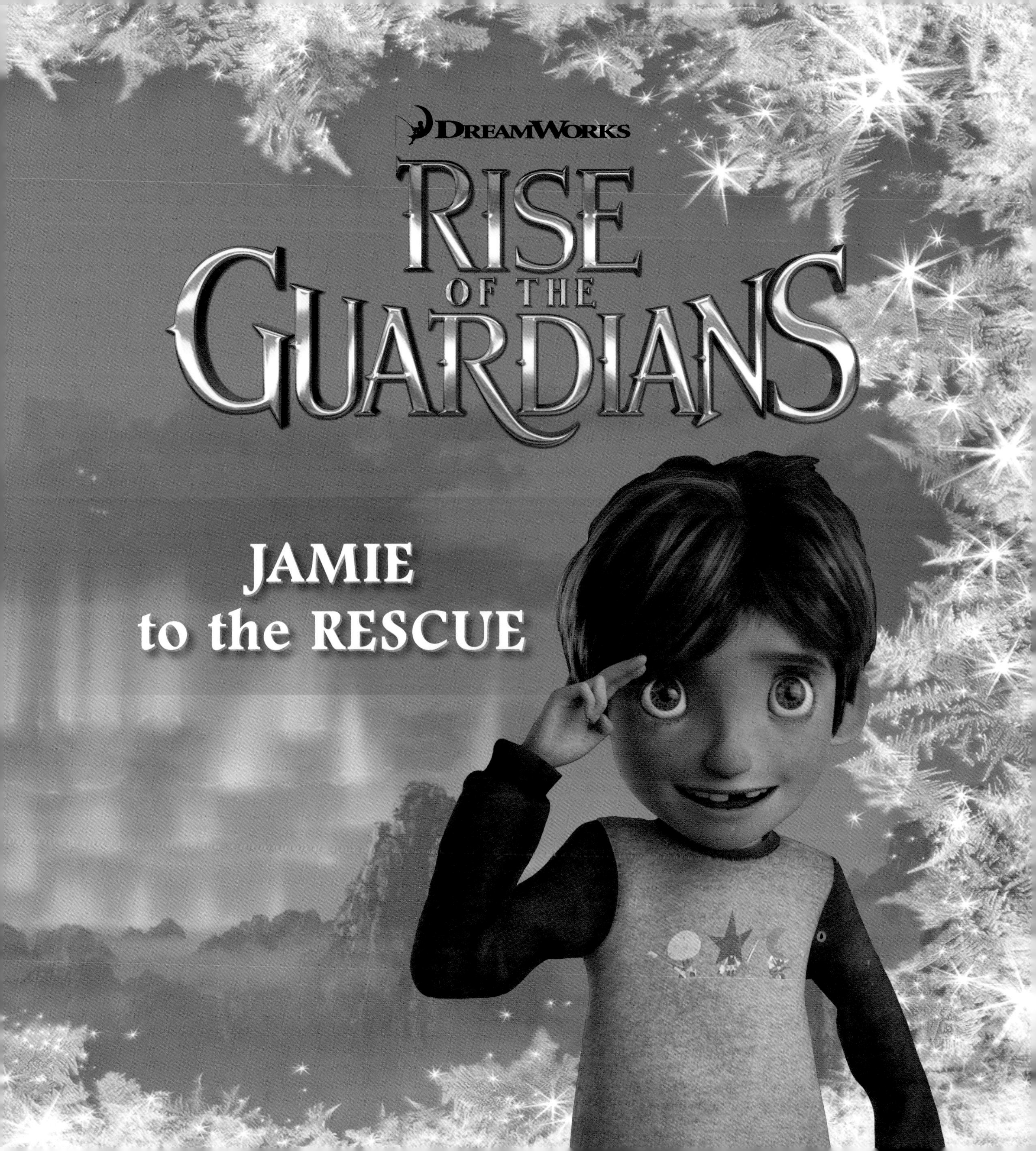
DreamWorks
RISE OF THE GUARDIANS
JAMIE
to the RESCUE

Jamie Bennett loves reading stories about mysteries and the unexplained. Little does he know that his ordinary life is about to become extraordinary!

MYSTERIOUS TIMES
THEY'RE OUT THERE !
moth monster
ET
chupacabra
sasquatch
lochness monster
yeti
SCIENCE . EXPLORATION . INNOVATION . FORENSICS
MYSTERIOUS TIMES
Other books in this series
Insects
birds
inventors
explorers
zoos
astronomy
the universe
the human body
weapons
religions
great migrations
trains
machines
airplanes

On his walk home from school one day, a snowball hits Jamie right in the back of his head.

POW! When he turns around, there isn't anyone near him. Which of his friends threw it? Where did it come from?

What Jamie doesn't know is that Jack Frost threw it. Jamie can't see Jack Frost...yet.

It doesn't really matter who started the fight. Now it is an all-out war! No matter how fast Jamie throws his snowballs, he never seems to run out. It's the best snowball fight ever!

Jack Frost leads the way as Jamie and his friends slide down a hill. He blasts a path of ice behind him.
It's very slippery…

Wheee! Jamie zips and zags through the town on his sled. He goes very fast—faster than he's ever gone before.

He doesn't see that Jack Frost is with him the entire way.

Jack Frost creates a huge ice ramp. It launches Jamie up and over the statue in the center of town. Jamie loves every minute of the ride!

When Jamie's sled finally lands, his friends gather around him and ask if he's okay.

Jamie smiles and holds up a tooth! That means the tooth fairy is coming!

That night, while Jamie is asleep, Jack Frost and Tooth come to his bedroom to collect his lost tooth and leave a coin.

But while Tooth is taking Jamie's tooth, the other Guardians burst through Jamie's window!

Tonight, the Guardians are helping Tooth collect teeth because Pitch, the boogeyman, has captured her mini fairies!

Jamie wakes up and shines a flashlight at the foot of his bed. He is surrounded by Guardians!

Jamie is thrilled to see them and has so many questions!

But Jamie must go back to sleep. Sandy tosses his dreamsand at Jamie, but it accidentally hits the other Guardians and they all fall asleep!

Jamie laughs at the sight of North, Bunny, and Tooth sound asleep on his floor.

Sandy sprinkles dreamsand directly on Jamie, and soon he is asleep, too.

On Easter Sunday, Jamie searches for Easter eggs. He is excited to see what goodies Bunny delivered. But he can't find anything.

Jamie wonders what has happened to Bunny. He's sure it wasn't a dream when he saw the Guardians by his bed.

XFB

Later that night, Jamie is alone in his room. He is talking to his favorite stuffed rabbit. He says he needs proof in order to keep believing.

Jack Frost has been listening outside of Jamie's window. He wants Jamie to believe! He ices the window and then draws a picture of an Easter egg and a rabbit.

Jamie can see Jack now. Jack is so excited that he makes it snow in Jamie's room! Jamie keeps believing in the Guardians!

The Guardians return to Jamie's town. Jamie learns that Pitch and his Nightmares have made children stop believing. He is the last child who still believes in the Guardians and they need his help.

Pitch tries to frighten Jamie. But Jamie stands up to Pitch. "I believe in you," he says. "I'm just not afraid of you."

Jamie and Jack start a snowball fight with Pitch! Jamie discovers that when his snowballs hit the Nightmares, they turn into golden dreamsand!

Dreamsand swirls through the town, turning everyone's nightmares back into beautiful dreams.

Jamie wakes up his friends by hitting their windows with snowballs. They all run outside and join in a snowball fight against Pitch. No one is afraid of him anymore.

The Guardians thank Jamie for helping them defeat Pitch. Jamie asks Jack if he will ever see him again. Jack tells Jamie the Guardians will always be in his heart—which kind of makes him a Guardian, too.

I even make winter boots look good.
¡Feliz Navidad, amigos!

Stocking stuffer duty.
I am so ready
for this mission.

DreamWorks' The Penguins of Madagascar

nickelodeon

# THE ALL-NIGHTER BEFORE CHRISTMAS

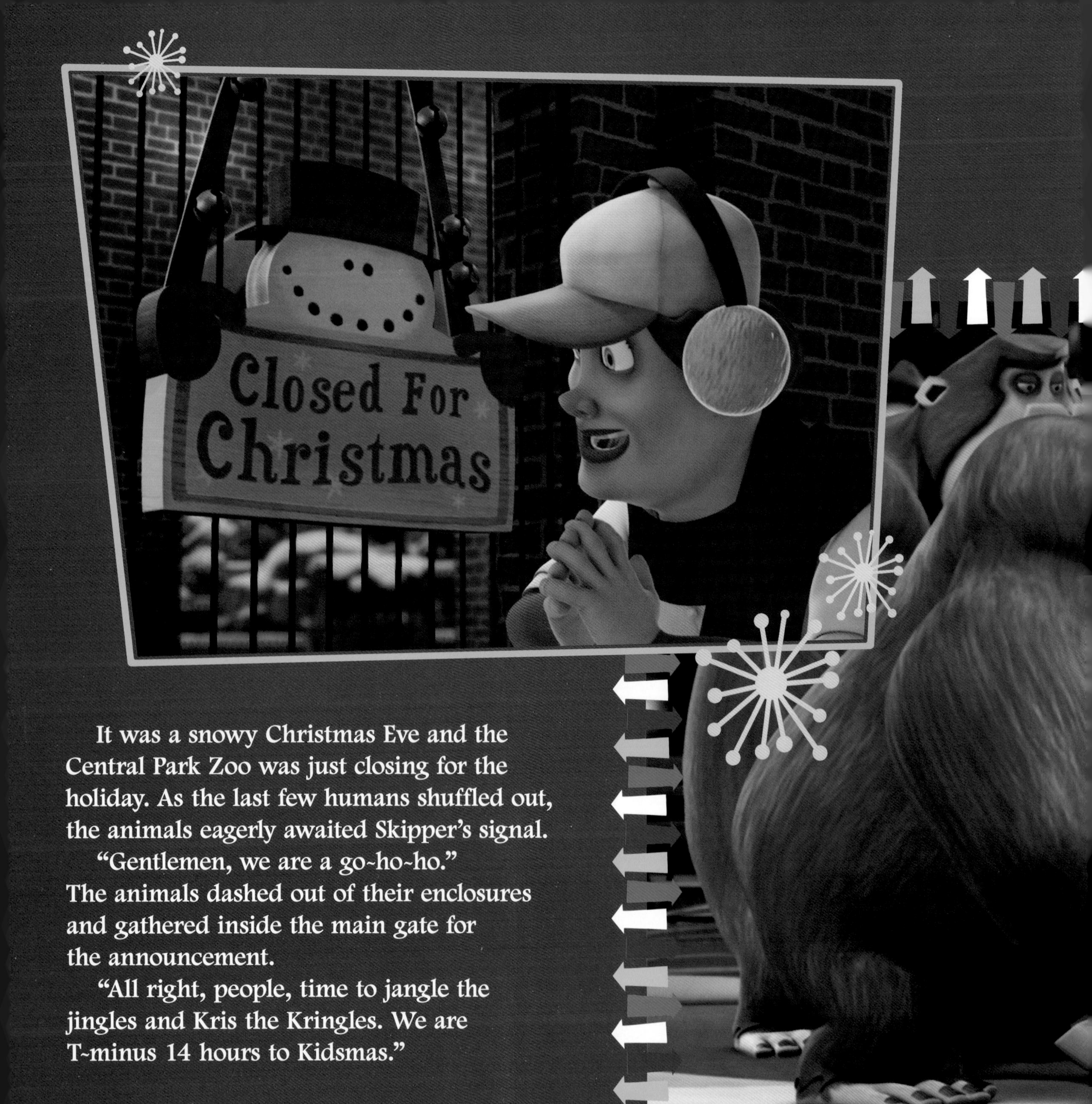


It was a snowy Christmas Eve and the Central Park Zoo was just closing for the holiday. As the last few humans shuffled out, the animals eagerly awaited Skipper's signal.

"Gentlemen, we are a go~ho~ho." The animals dashed out of their enclosures and gathered inside the main gate for the announcement.

"All right, people, time to jangle the jingles and Kris the Kringles. We are T~minus 14 hours to Kidsmas."

The little ducklings, possums, and raccoons jumped up and down, waving their wings and paws.

"But not till morning," Private reminded. The excited baby animals reluctantly crawled home.

"So, 'Kidsmas.' This relates to Christmas how exactly?" asked Roger the alligator.

“Every year the Central Park Zoo closes from Christmas Eve to December 26,” Kowalski explained. “We take advantage of this human-free environment to throw a mondo Christmas fiesta called Kidsmas for the animal families.”

Skipper jumped in. “You know the drill, people. Open those assignment cards, and let’s make this a great Kidsmas.”

King Julien pushed through the animals holding up his assignment card, the same one as last year.

"Who do I give a talking to if my job is stupid and lame?" he demanded.

Private was surprised. "Children love the gingerbread house."

"They also love finding crusty things in their noses," Julien responded. "I am a king! I demand the most important of all Kidsmas tasks!"

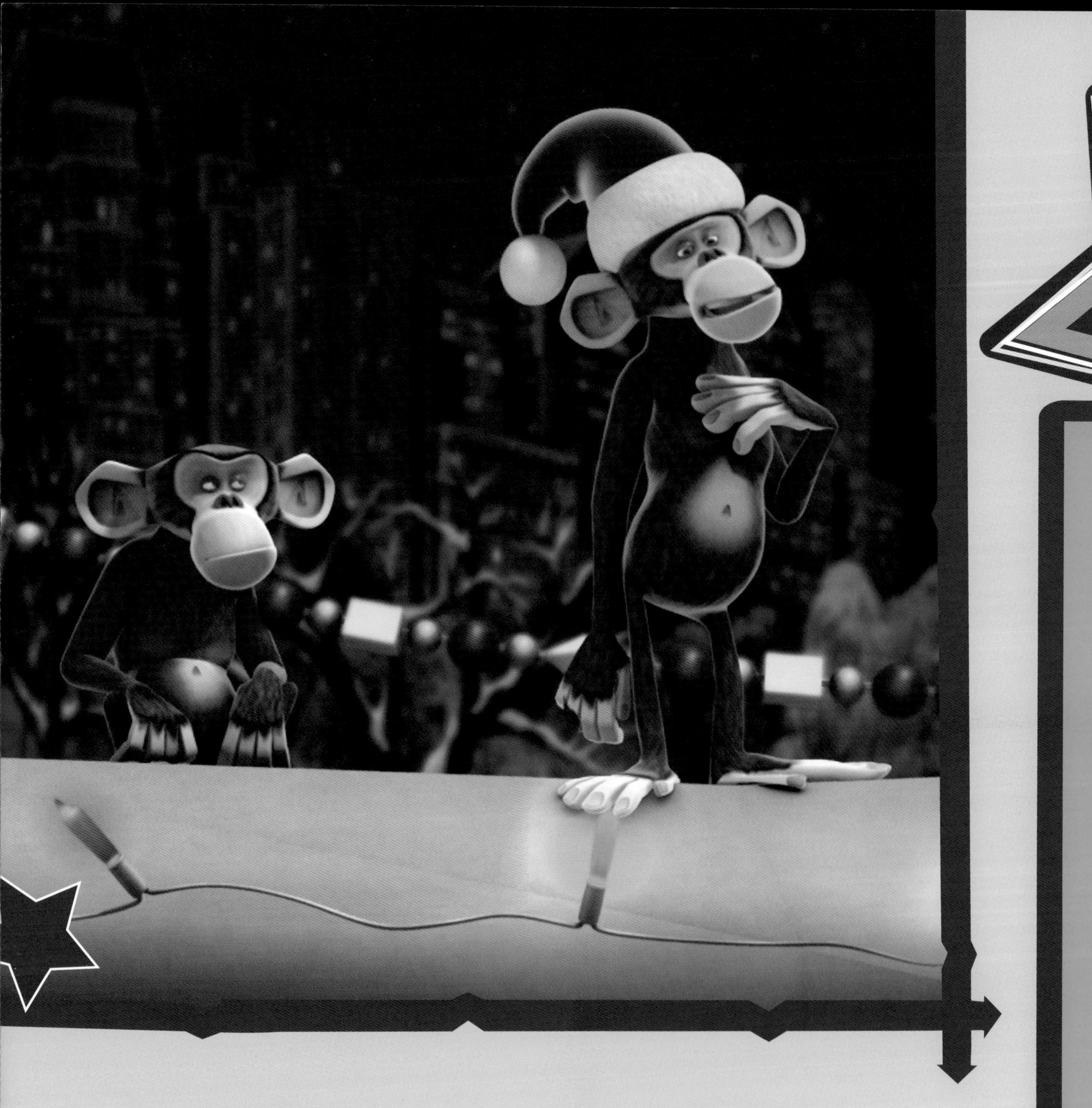

Skipper denied Julien's request. "Kidsmas is a well-oiled machine with years of tradition." That was true. Burt always makes his famous peanut nog. Mason always dresses up as zoo Santa. And so on. "We're not swapping assignments the night before the big event," Skipper commanded. "End of story."

“What happened to the freedom of changing?” Julien protested. The animals decided he had a point. They, too, were tired of doing the same task every year.

“We’re on an overnight deadline, people! There’s no time to—” Skipper started when Julien snatched all the cards. Against Skipper’s wishes, the animals swapped assignments.

Julien chose a very important job: find the Christmas tree. Then Private announced Skipper would be Santa, the *most* important task. The exasperated king twitched with jealousy.

Meanwhile, Marlene, Rico and Phil were thrilled to be decorating. So were Mason, Burt and Kowalski. Both committees had very different ideas about what the decoration theme should be.

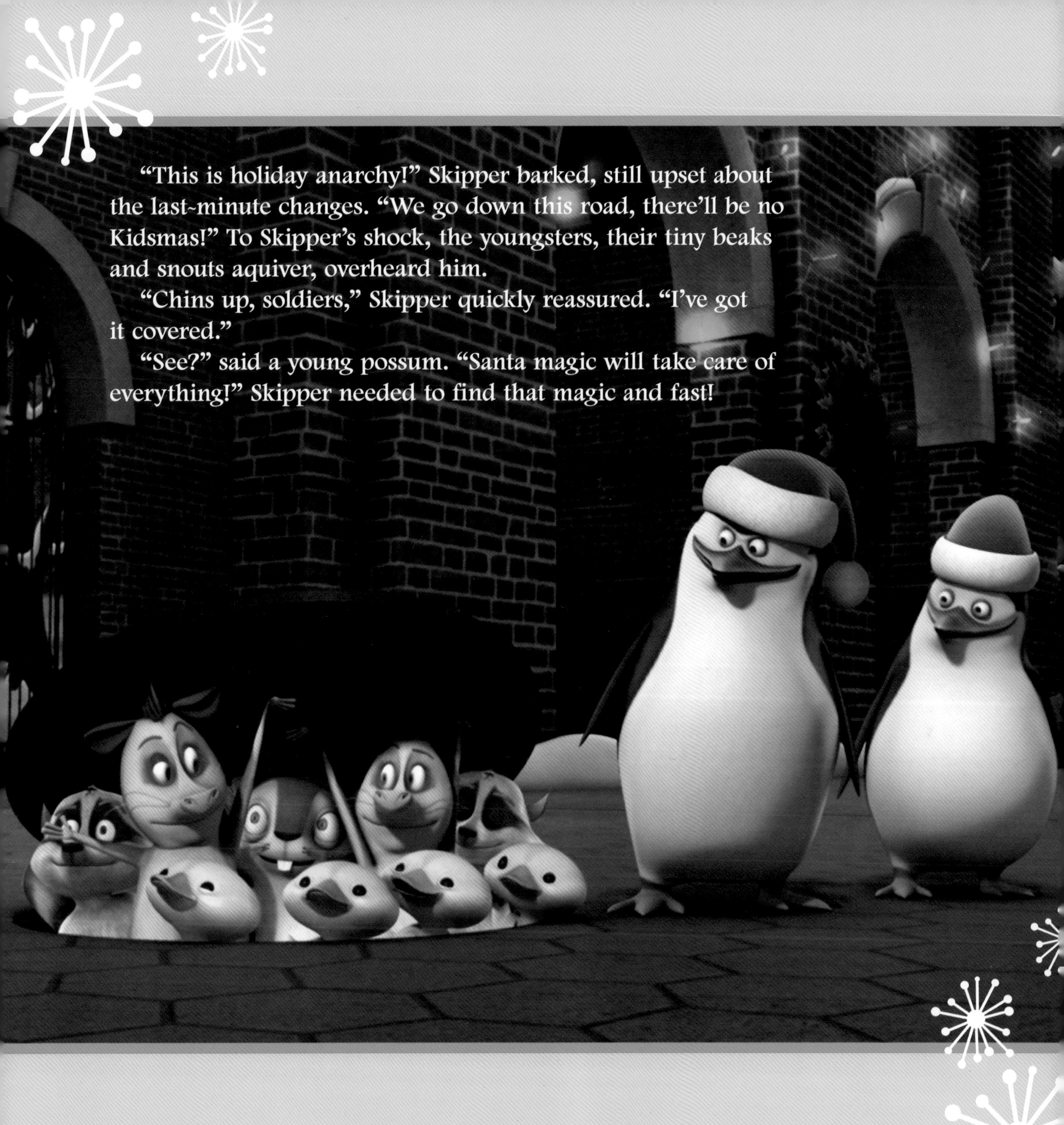

"This is holiday anarchy!" Skipper barked, still upset about the last-minute changes. "We go down this road, there'll be no Kidsmas!" To Skipper's shock, the youngsters, their tiny beaks and snouts aquiver, overheard him.

"Chins up, soldiers," Skipper quickly reassured. "I've got it covered."

"See?" said a young possum. "Santa magic will take care of everything!" Skipper needed to find that magic and fast!

All the animals got to work. Bada, Bing, and the iguanas were excited to lead the music. Roger sat down at the piano to orchestrate the band.

"La~la~lo~la~lo~la~loooooo," bellowed Bada and Bing as the iguanas screeched. Roger cringed at the caterwauling. No wonder this group was not usually in charge of the Kidsmas music.

Meanwhile, Skipper and Private searched for Santa magic.
"Curse you, Internet! Twenty-eight thousand cat videos, zero useful information!" Skipper huffed. "If Mr. Tub of Jolly has some sparkly mystic secret, I need to find it ASAP!"
Private piped up with a solution. "If you want real Santa magic, we should ask Santa!"

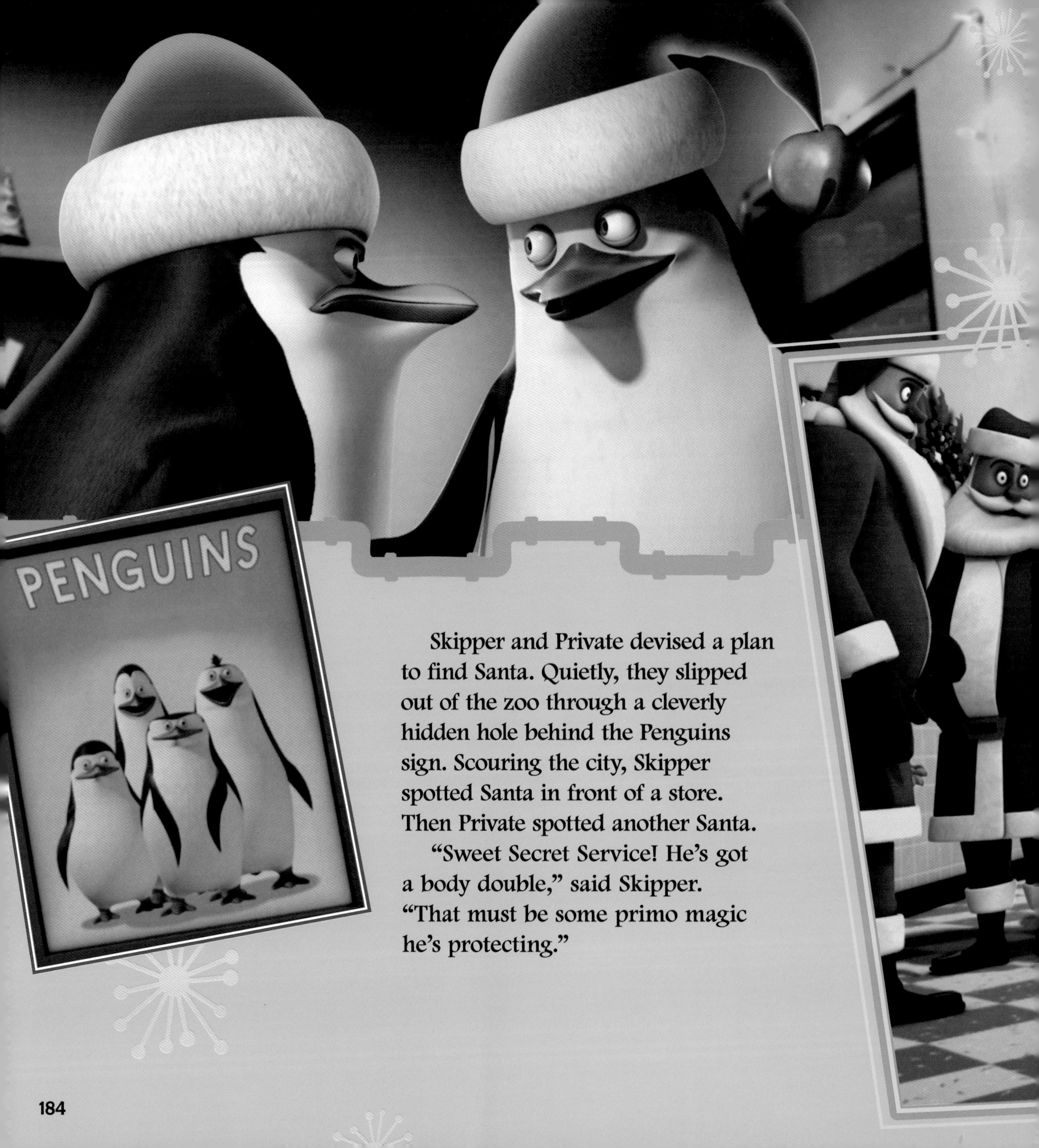


Skipper and Private devised a plan to find Santa. Quietly, they slipped out of the zoo through a cleverly hidden hole behind the Penguins sign. Scouring the city, Skipper spotted Santa in front of a store. Then Private spotted another Santa.

"Sweet Secret Service! He's got a body double," said Skipper. "That must be some primo magic he's protecting."

"They're leaving!" cried Private.

"No time to I.D. which Papa Noel is the phony," Skipper determined. Each penguin followed one Santa. Curiously, they led to the same place. And there weren't just two phonies, but a room full of fake Santas.

"Wind-up monkey misdirect!" Skipper ordered. The penguins pretended to be animated toys, exiting the room without suspicion.

Elsewhere in New York City, Julien searched for a tree. Nothing Maurice found was good enough.

"The flavor of the tree is not the problem," groaned Julien. "It is the not-importance of it!"

"I thought this was the most important job," said Mort.

"It was, until the flathead penguin got a better one. Now we must find the *amazingest* tree in the history of Kidsmas!"

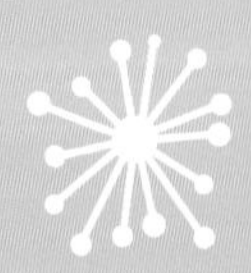

They searched and searched until Maurice was worn out. "We've seen real trees, fake trees and you keep turning your nose at all of them."

"I need a tree that sits up, smacks you upon the face, and says, 'Christmas!'" demanded Julien.

Maurice handed him one last tree. "This one says it in seventeen languages." Julien was still not satisfied.

Then Julien's eyes grew large. Just beyond a crowd of humans stood the biggest, brightest, most decorated tree in all of New York City.

"Finally, a tree amazing enough to beat the Santa penguin," Julien declared. "Choppity chop with the chopping!"

Mort got to work. Julien needed this tree at the zoo in time for Kidsmas.

Meanwhile, Roger tried to keep the music performance on track. The iguanas were willing to practice but didn't always understand Roger's instructions. Plus, they sounded awful. To make matters worse, Bada and Bing were writing their *own* music.

"Fellas, we're on a tight schedule here..." urged Roger. He backed off when Bada began beating his chest.

Things weren't faring any better among the two decorating committees. Marlene, Phil, and Rico went with a rock 'n' roll theme, which clashed with the more refined style that Mason, Kowalski, and Burt had assembled.

"Guys?" asked Marlene. "What are you doing?"

"Our jobs, obviously," Mason answered haughtily.

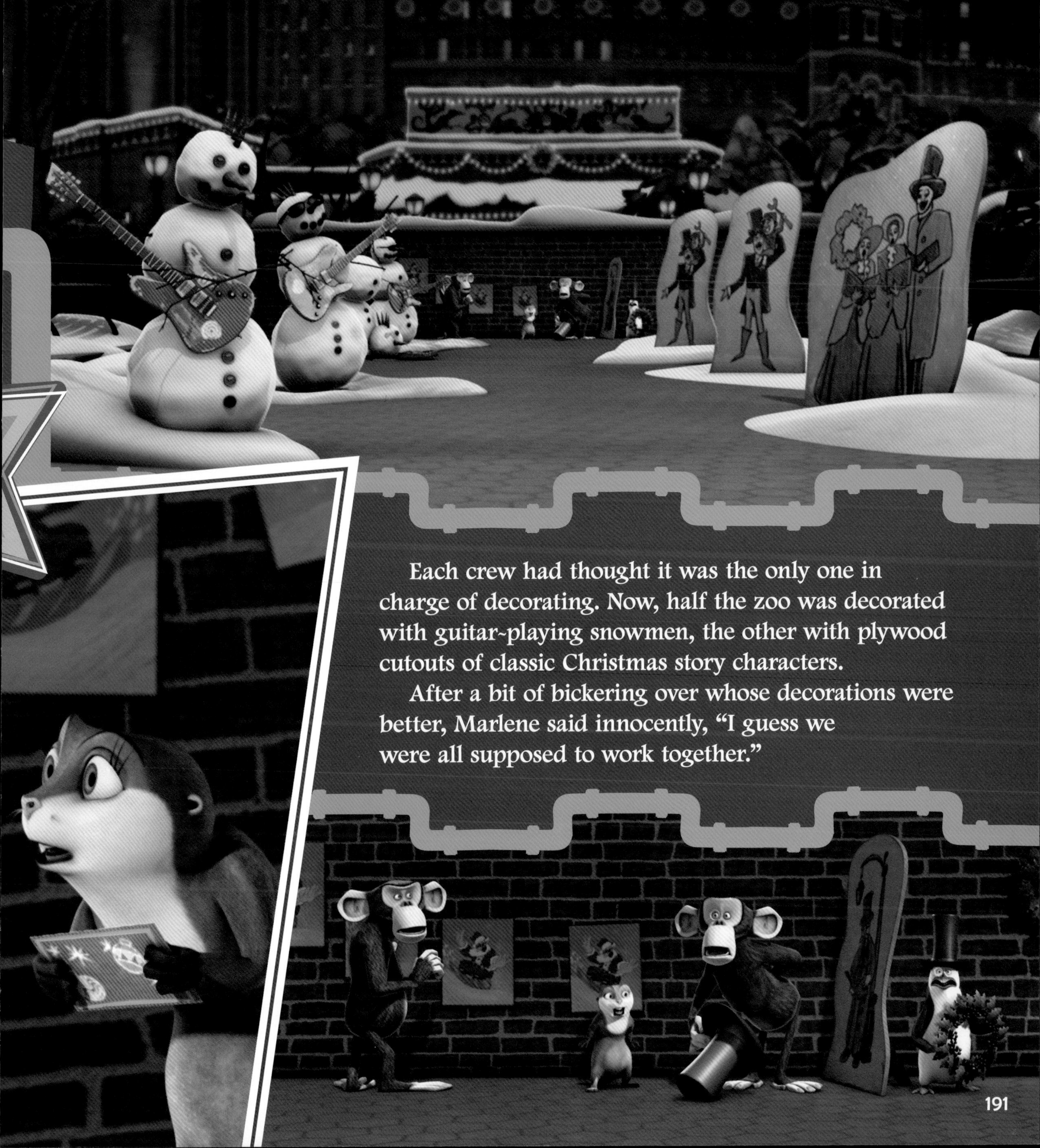

Each crew had thought it was the only one in charge of decorating. Now, half the zoo was decorated with guitar-playing snowmen, the other with plywood cutouts of classic Christmas story characters.

After a bit of bickering over whose decorations were better, Marlene said innocently, “I guess we were all supposed to work together.”

But neither decorating crew wanted to give up their decorations in favor of the others'.

"How do we solve this?" Marlene asked hopefully.

Kowalski suggested, "Elephant rules." With that, his crewmate, Burt the elephant, squashed all the rock 'n' roll snowmen. That triggered a wild snowball battle between the crews, during which both teams' decorations were ruined.

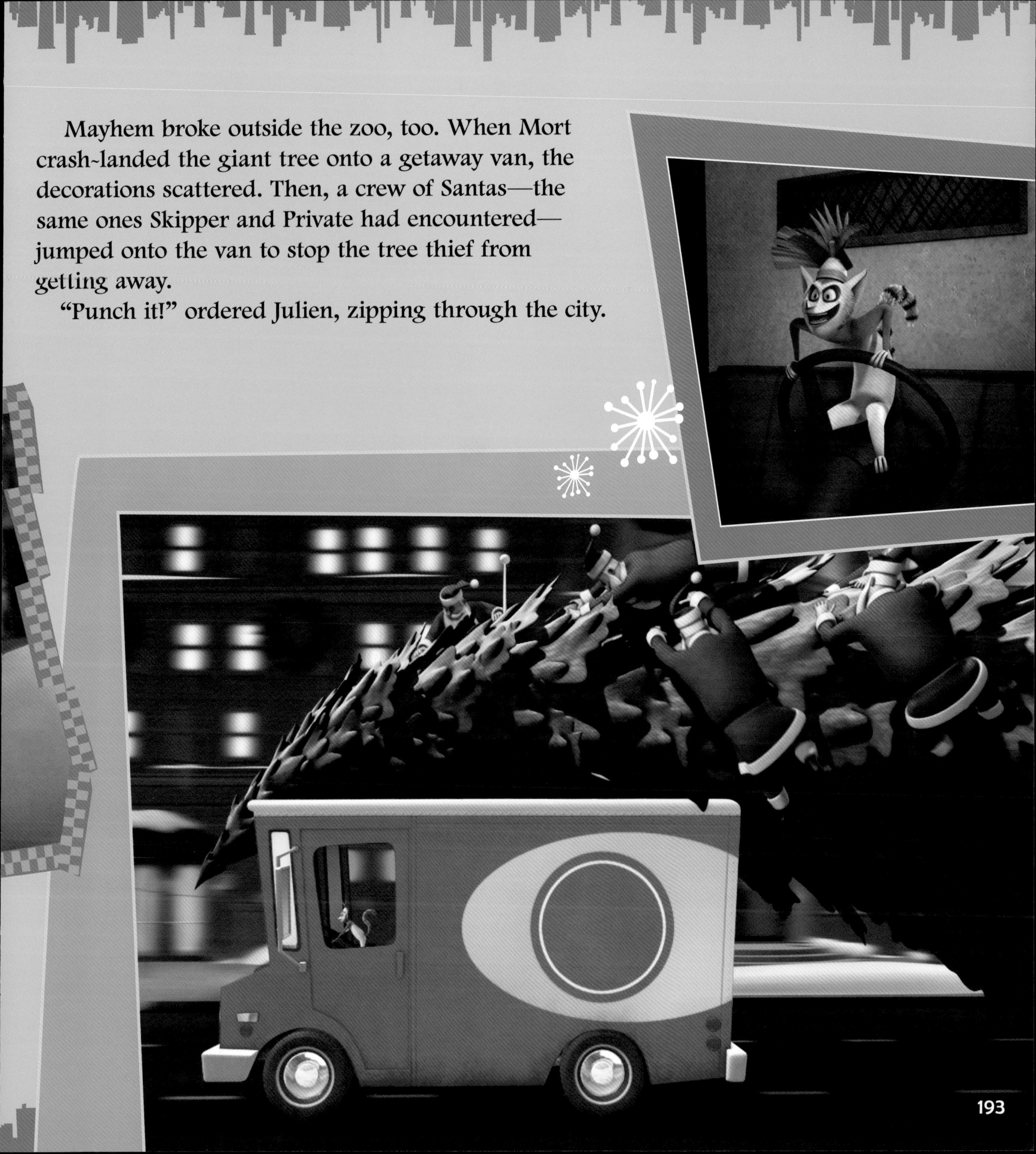

Mayhem broke outside the zoo, too. When Mort crash-landed the giant tree onto a getaway van, the decorations scattered. Then, a crew of Santas—the same ones Skipper and Private had encountered—jumped onto the van to stop the tree thief from getting away.

"Punch it!" ordered Julien, zipping through the city.

The van whizzed past Skipper. Seeing all those Santas, but not Julien, he thought the real Santa was escaping.

"The imposters are trying to haul him back in," Skipper reasoned. "Execute mobile rescue op!"

Swinging like Tarzan on a strand of holiday lights, Skipper and Private landed on the tree. One by one, the penguins dispatched the fake Santas.

The final phony Father Christmas crawled toward the cab, reaching for the animals.

"Abandon van," ordered Julien. "We must save the tree!" The penguins and lemurs leapt onto the van roof as fake Santa took the wheel. When the van stopped short, the tree—and the animals—soared through the air across town, miraculously landing inside the zoo!

Skipper scowled at the messy zoo and bickering animals. "Fa-la-la-la-la-la-boo-hoo-hoo! Didn't I warn you people? I can't leave you alone for one night—" Skipper paused as Eggy the duckling approached.

"You promised this would be the best Kidsmas," he sniffed. The big animals felt bad, but Skipper took all the blame.

"I'm the Santa here. This was on my watch."

Just then, the merry tinkling of jingle bells filled the air and a magical sparkle of lights appeared overhead. It was the real Santa! And he was not happy about the mess the animals had made across the city.

"All I wanted was a tiny taste of that real Santa magic," said Skipper.

Before flying off again, Santa said, "But Skipper, you had that from the beginning."

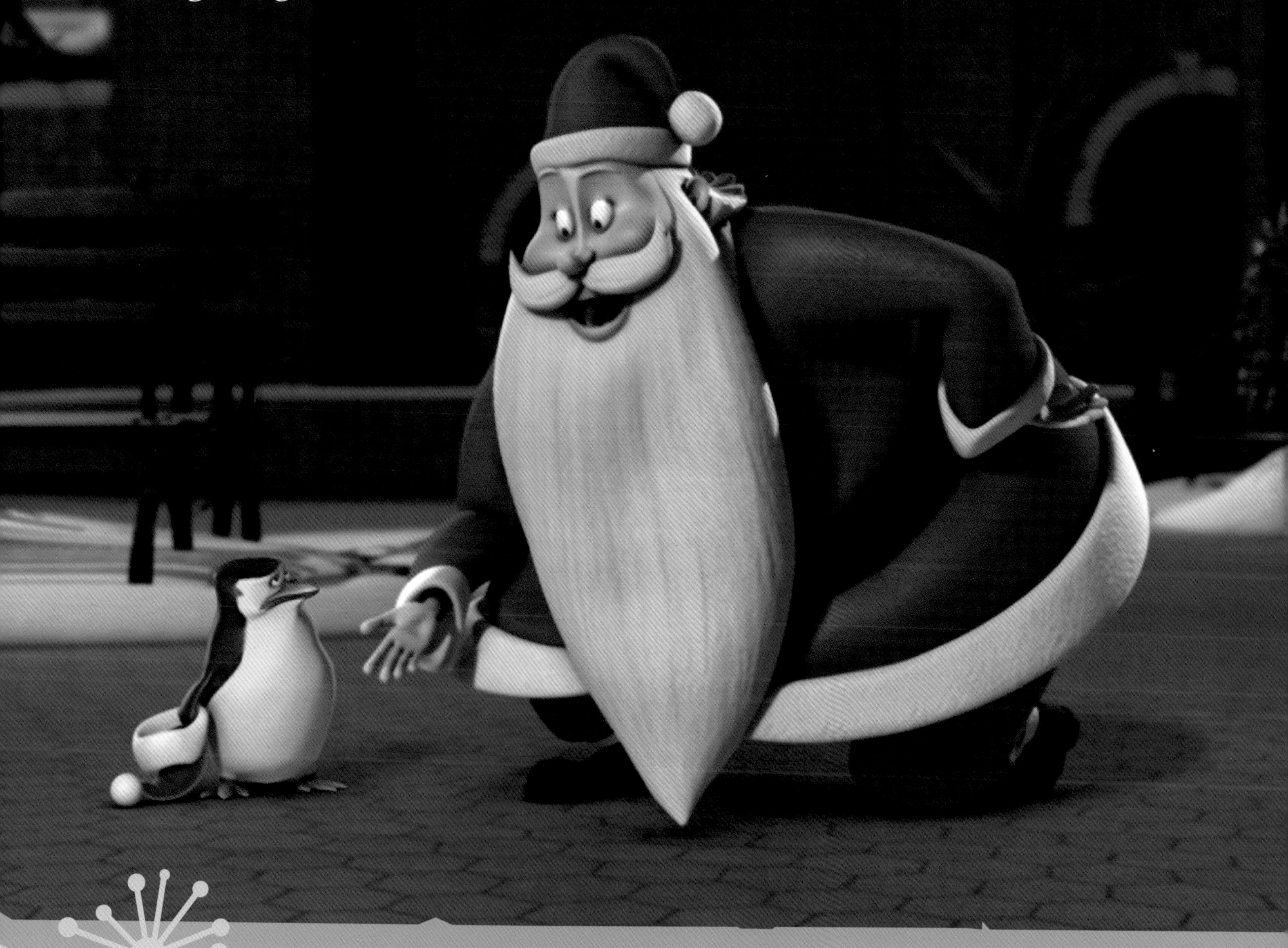

“What do you suppose Santa meant?” asked Private.

Skipper thought a moment. His body started to tingle.

“Santa magic...coursing through veins. Feels...gingerbready. Follow my lead, people!” Skipper called for holiday music. Bada and Bing sang their new song. Though they were off key and the lyrics weren’t finished, it was still filled with holiday spirit.

*"So what if you didn't get all your Christmas wishes,"* sang the gorillas. *"There ain't another day that's a better one than this is."*

*Private chimed in, "So Santa skipped the best things that were on your list."* *"But soldier, tell those frowns to cease and desist,"* Skipper finished with a smile.

*"If you know where to look, you'll find your Christmas bliss,"* lilted Marlene.

*"We'll sing it one more time, maybe you will catch the gist,"* Julien crooned.

The joyful song even inspired the dueling decorators to put their differences aside. The two crews worked together and came up with a fun Christmas style all their own.

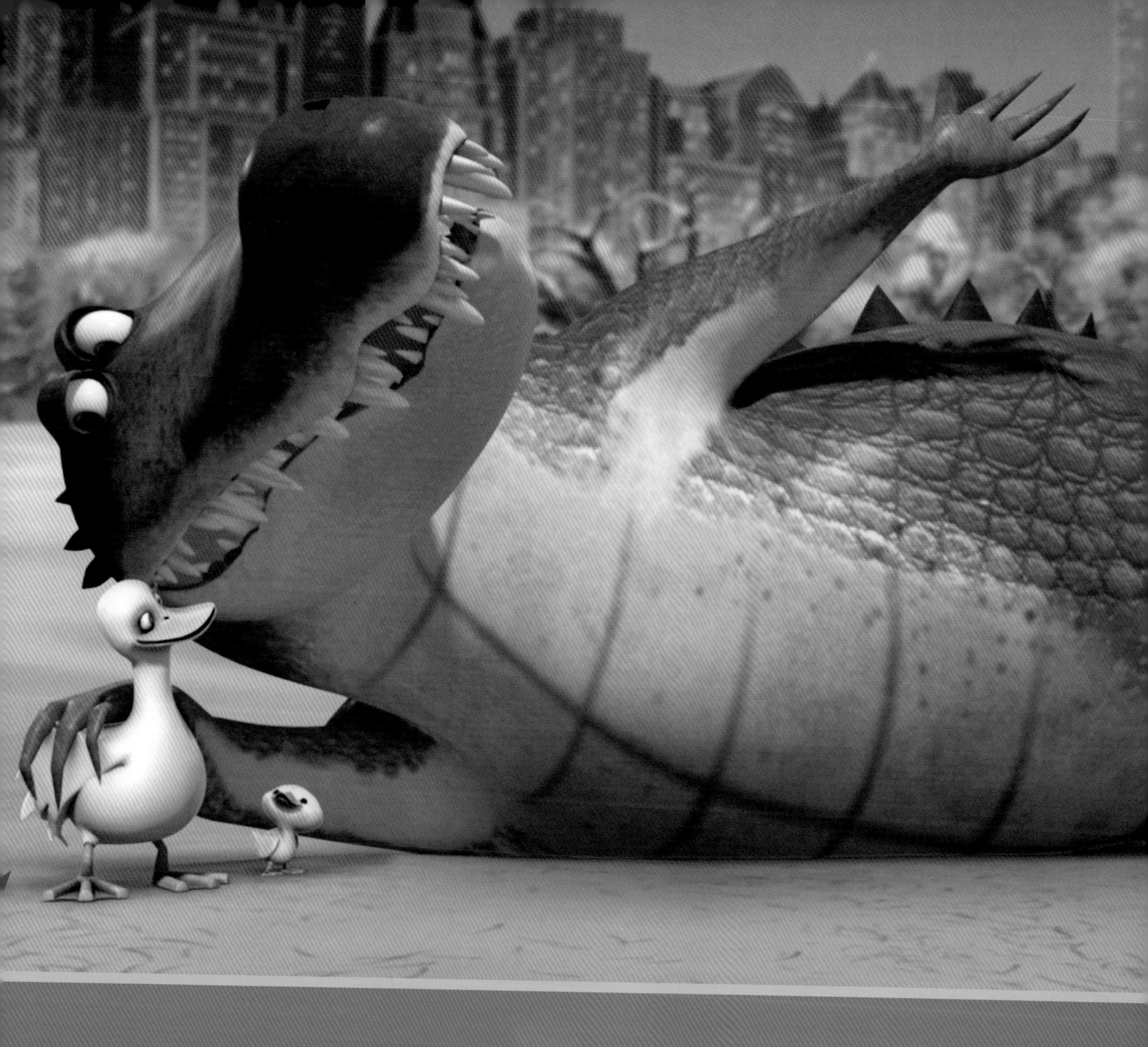

*"It ain't perfect but it's Christmas, so what if your day's had a few minor glitches," warbled the zoo friends.*

*"Just clean up the mess and help your mom with the dishes," Roger belted.*

*"'Cause, kids, it ain't perfect, but it's still Christmas. Christmas. Christmas. Christmas. Christmas."*

Santa magic was everywhere—even around Julien's Christmas tree, which lit up the night.

"You really did it!" exclaimed Private. "You found the Santa magic. What was the secret?"

"No secret, Private," Skipper replied. "Big Red was right—we had to get back to where this all started: trying to make some kids happy for Christmas."

"That's it? Santa magic is just making people happy?"

"It seems to work for that guy," said Skipper as Santa flew overhead one last time before his big delivery of the year.

Eggy was so happy he hugged Skipper. "Merry Christmas, Mister Skipper Penguin." Kidsmas was restored at last and Skipper was quick to pass along the good will.

"And to all, a good night."

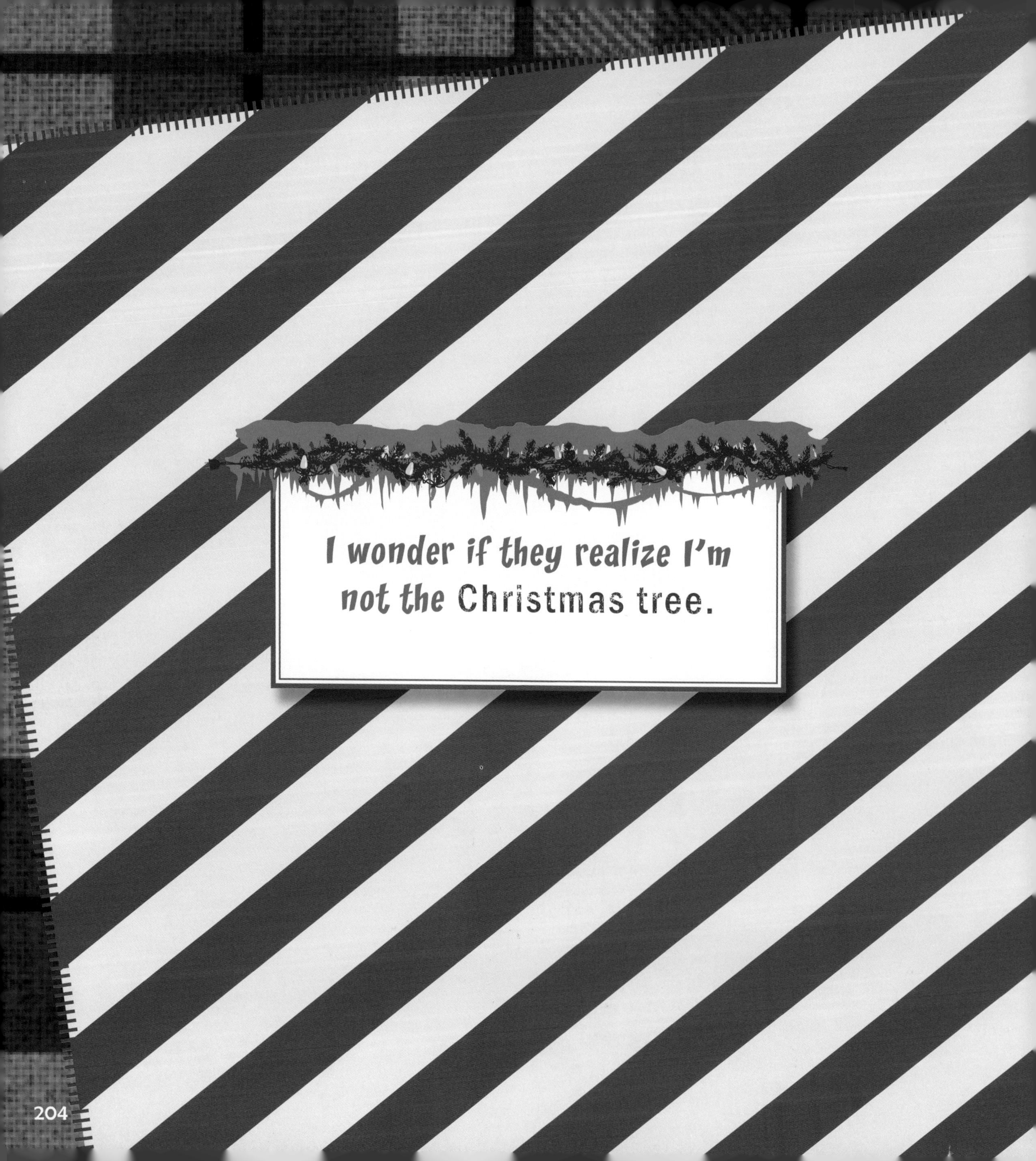
I wonder if they realize I'm not the Christmas tree.

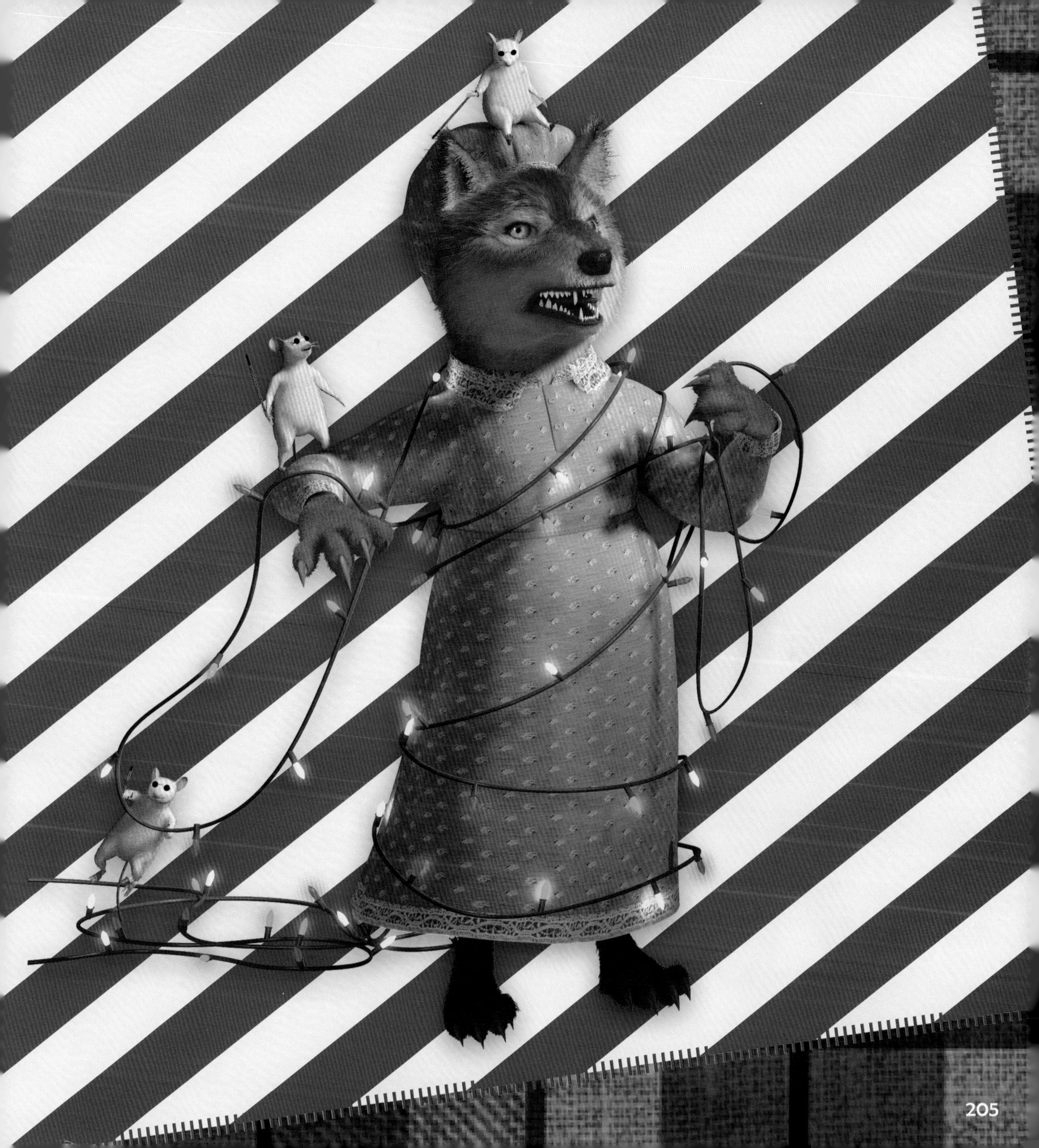

It should be Julianuary
all year long!

HAPPY NEW YEAR

DreamWorks
The Penguins of Madagascar
nickelodeon
SNOWMAGEDDON

It was the day of the super big game between the New York Behemoths and the Miami Mayhem.

"Got my pre-game hype, my super fan gear, and my tasty array of greasy, artery-clogging snacks!" Skipper told Marlene happily.

But Skipper hadn't planned on Rico's pre-game super snack attack!

"Oh great. Now we gotta execute another snack mission!" Skipper said. "C'mon, boys!"

"Actually, Skipper," Kowalski said, "Private and I are going to pass on the game."

According to Kowalski's research, fall was the perfect time to observe the annual end of photo-synthetic glucose production.

"Plus the leaves are so pretty!" Private enthused.

"All right, boys," Skipper said. "Report back on those leaves!"

PHOTOSYNTHETIC
PROCESSES

Kowalski and Private had just established their Fall Leaves Observation Post in the park when Fred dropped by to find out what was going on.

"We're watching the leaves change," Private explained.

"Oh. Wait. Change into what, though?" Fred asked.

Kowalski sighed.

Across the street at the Snackatarium, Skipper was leading Marlene on her first-ever snack retrieval mission.

"Welcome to nosh heaven, Marlene!" Skipper announced. "If it comes in a wrapper, carton, or screwtop they have it here!"

While Marlene eagerly scouted out the Slushuccino machine, Skipper came up with a plan of action.

"Let's start with the Sticky food group!" he commanded.

Suddenly, an urgent news bulletin blared from the TV.

"It's freakish and it's here," Gil Force warned ominously. "The storm of the century! If you are outside, get inside! And if you're inside, stay there, because THIS! IS! SNOWMAGEDDON!"

At that moment, Skipper and Marlene realized they had more immediate problems than Snowmageddon.

Their arch-nemesis X—as in former Animal Control, Exterminator, Temporary Zookeeper, Fishmonger Officer X—was in the building! It was only a matter of time before they were discovered.

Things weren't looking so great outside either.

"Precipitous precipitation," Kowalski said as the snow began to fall. "Perhaps we should head back before..." With a gasp, Kowalski grabbed the camera to get a better view of the Snackatarium.

"GAAH! It's X!" Kowalski shouted.

"He's in there with Skipper?" Private exclaimed. "We've got to..."

WHOOMP!

Snowmageddon walloped everything in sight with an icy blast of white!

Kowalski, Private, and Fred were tossed . . . and tumbled . . . and bumped . . . and jumbled . . . until they finally came to rest inside a big, sheltering tree.

Piles of hard-packed snow blocked the exit.

“We’re not getting out of here anytime soon, are we?” Private asked.

“No,” Kowalski replied glumly.

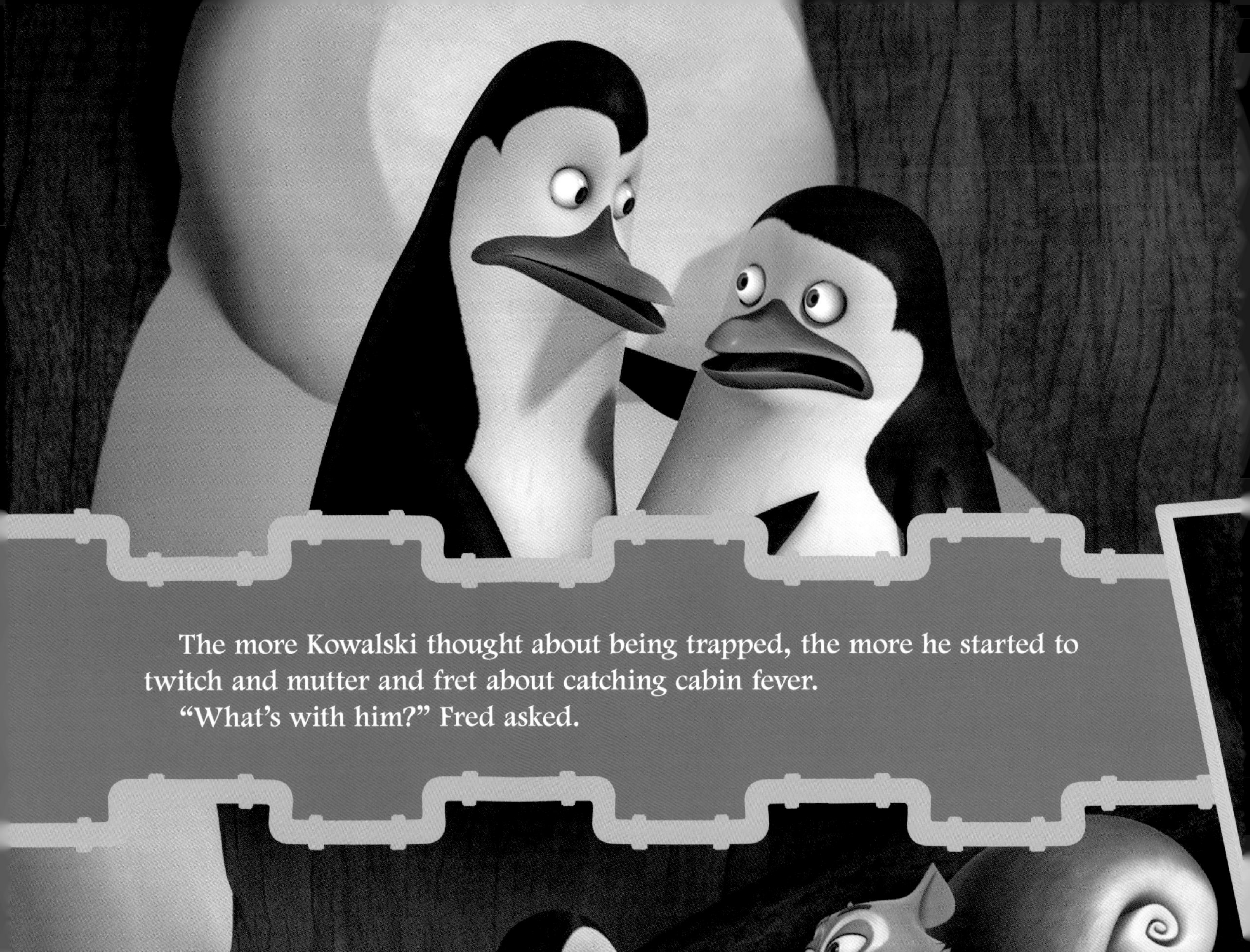

The more Kowalski thought about being trapped, the more he started to twitch and mutter and fret about catching cabin fever.

"What's with him?" Fred asked.

Private explained that Kowalski was desperate to get out so they could rescue Skipper.

"Oh," said Fred, chomping on an acorn. "Why don't you just go out through the basement?"

Basement? There was a basement? A split second later, Kowalski and Private were out of there!

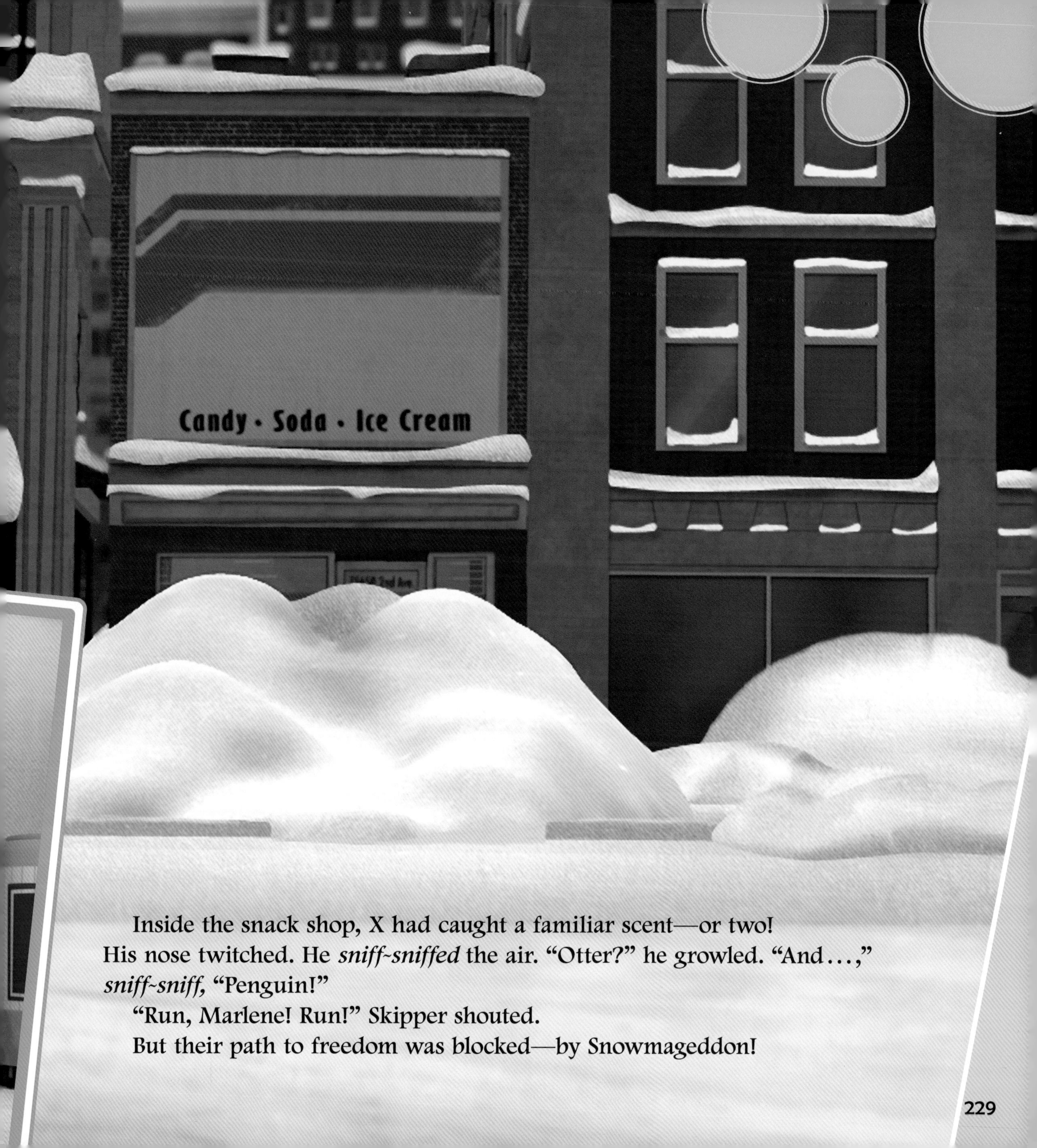


Inside the snack shop, X had caught a familiar scent—or two! His nose twitched. He *sniff-sniffed* the air. "Otter?" he growled. "And...," *sniff-sniff,* "Penguin!"

"Run, Marlene! Run!" Skipper shouted.

But their path to freedom was blocked—by Snowmageddon!

Skipper and Marlene dodged and hid, tricked and taunted, slid and skittered—but X was hot on their heels. Just as they were about to make a bold escape through a strategically high window, X nabbed Skipper!

Marlene quickly ducked out of sight. With Skipper in a big-time bind, it was up to her to come up with a plan.

While X was on the phone with Animal Control, Marlene got busy stuffing the Slushuccino machine with every juice-able item she could find.

"I'd trudge through a hundred blizzards to deliver you to justice," X told Skipper gleefully.

"If you're gonna do that, be sure to hydrate," Marlene called out from her perch on the super-charged Slushuccino machine.

Marlene pulled the lever, and the machine blasted a path clear out of the snack shop!

It was a brilliant operation—until X captured them both just outside the store!

Suddenly—BAM!—a heavy metal manhole cover hurtled into the air and landed with a bone-crunching thud on X's foot.

"OOOWWWW! OOOOOW!" X bellowed as Skipper and Marlene turned the tables with a couple of well-executed moves.

By the time Private and Kowalski jumped out of the manhole ready for action, Skipper and Marlene had already saved the day!

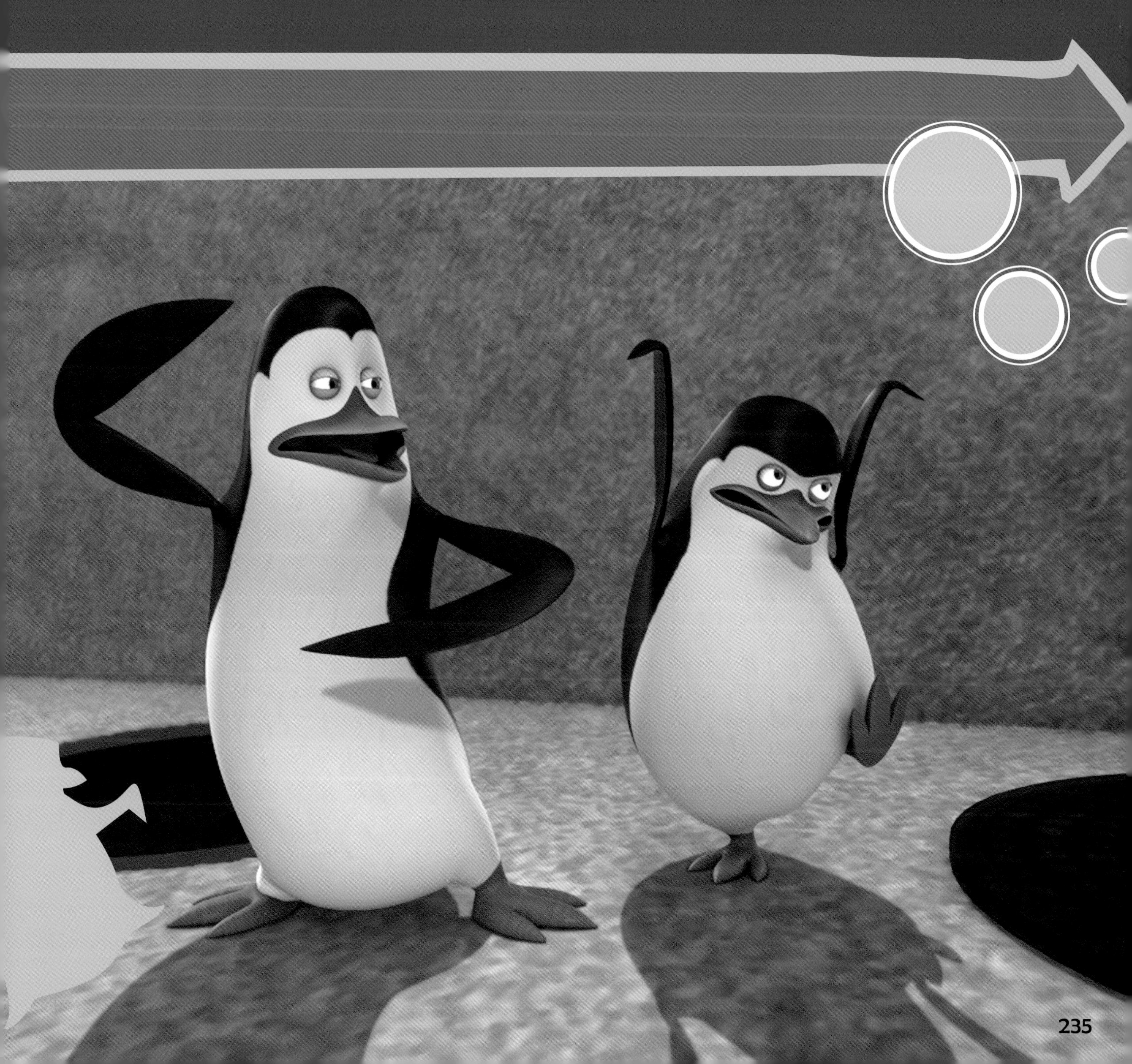

"Now let's get home so I can at least see the end of the game," said Skipper.

"Wow! A real nail-biter! Never have I seen a more exciting finish!" the TV anchor announced just as Skipper entered the room. Rico was cheering wildly.

Skipper looked around. Oh, well. He might have missed the super big game, but his team had taken on Snowmageddon—and pulled off a super big win.

The best part about Christmas is sharing something special with your special someone. I can't wait to see Shrek's face when he opens my gift: festering swamp eel eggs!

I've got Christmas
all wrapped up.

TO:
FROM:

# OPERATION ANTARCTICA

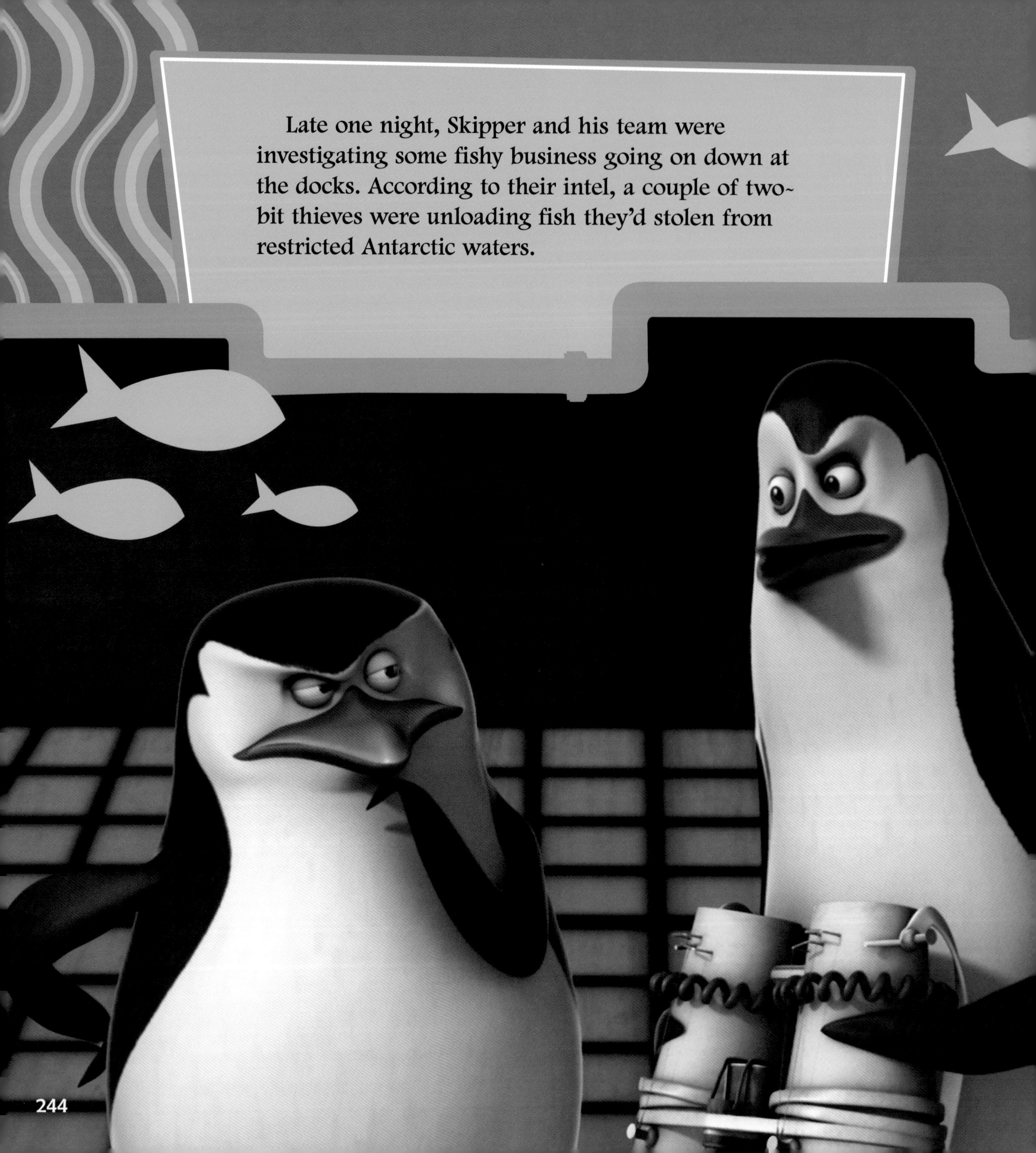

Late one night, Skipper and his team were investigating some fishy business going on down at the docks. According to their intel, a couple of two-bit thieves were unloading fish they'd stolen from restricted Antarctic waters.

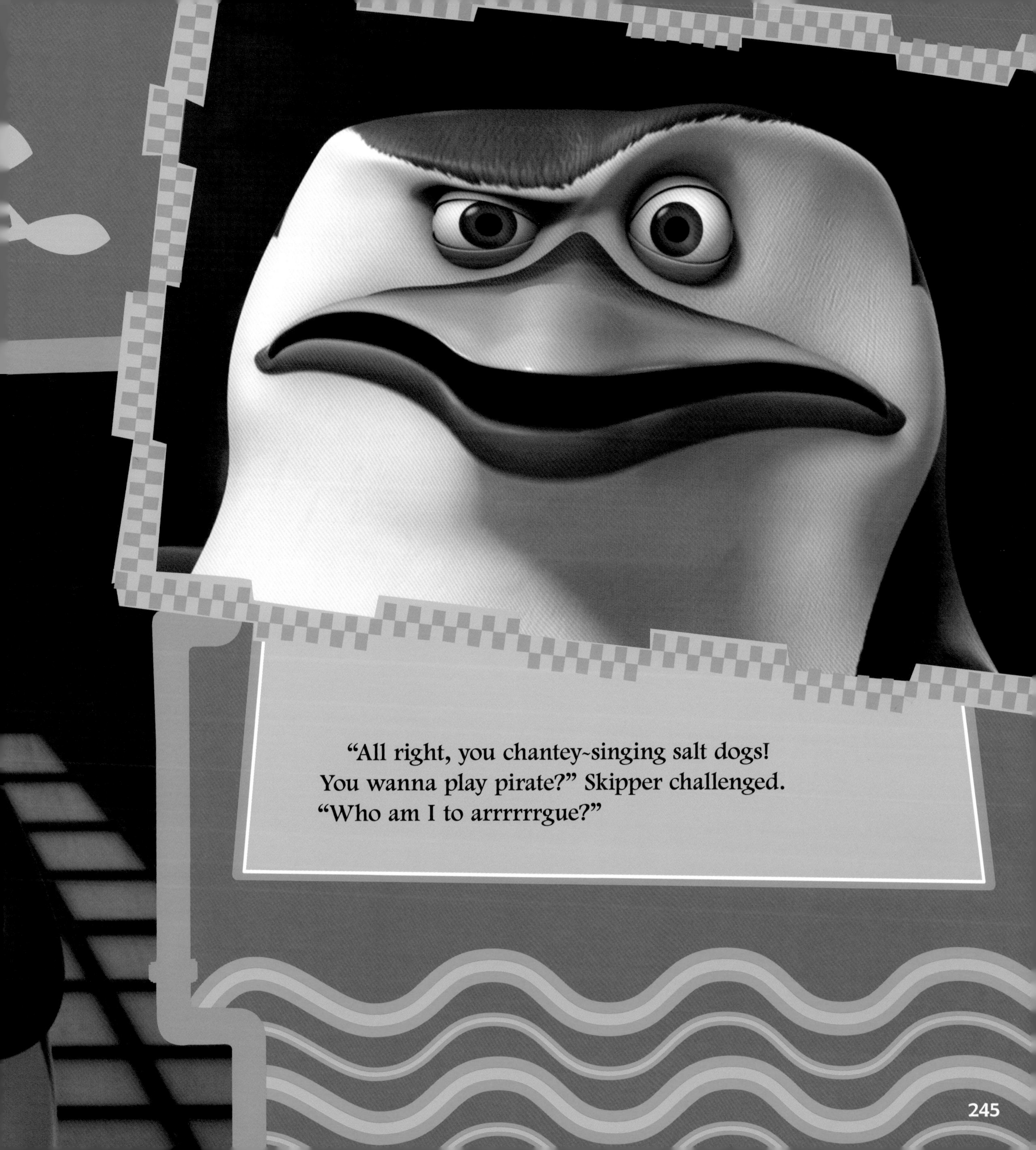

"All right, you chantey-singing salt dogs! You wanna play pirate?" Skipper challenged. "Who am I to arrrrrrgue?"

The silent, shadowy docks erupted in shouts of "Ahoy! Avast! En garde!"—not to mention grunts and crashes and groans—as the swashbuckling good-guy Penguin Pirates took down, and tied up, the crusty pirate crooks.

Another successful mission! And just in time for the late-night news!

In all the excitement, no one but Private heard the tiny voice calling for help from the fish-stick processing tank.

Private scrambled to the top of the slippery slicing machine and promptly fell in. He landed with a slimy splat right next to—GAAK!—a leopard seal!

When the young predator snagged him, Private thought he was a goner. But then the seal pup threw him from the tank to safety! With no time to lose, Private cranked up an industrial crane to save his new friend from a decidedly dicey fate.

Pupnapped from Antarctica, Hunter the leopard seal just wanted to get back home.

Private did his best to enlist the team's help, but they weren't buying Hunter's claim that she was a strict "fishitarian." Kowalski insisted that it was only a matter of time before the seal pup developed a taste for penguin meat—and no self-respecting penguin wanted to be around for that particular developmental milestone!

"She's in trouble, Skipper," Private argued. "As penguins of honor, it's our duty to help."

"You should splash down somewhere in the East River," Kowalski told Hunter as they tied her to a catapult. "Then go south."

"She's only a pup!" Private objected. "She'll never make it to Antarctica on her own!"

Kowalski was already hitting the eject button when Private leaped onto the catapult. Before anyone could even say "Ooops!" both Private and Hunter were hurtling into the night!

The pair landed with an enormous splash in the East River, 8,523 miles from Antarctica.

"Boys, Private just hitched a ride on the Pinniped Express to New Deadburg," Skipper announced gravely. "We don't let a man swim into seal-infested waters alone—even our most naive man."

Without further ado, the team fired up the submarine and set a course for Antarctica.

By the time Skipper realized he also had a hitchhiker, it was too late to turn back. For better or for worse, Julien was now a member of their ridiculously risky rescue mission.

The psycho-seal attack on the submarine came out of the blue.

"Nice try!" Skipper taunted. "No tiny-brained seal skull can pound through six inches of steel!" Unfortunately, the tiny-brained seal skulls had no trouble pounding through glass. The sub began to sink!

Acting quickly, the team launched Julien, their unseaworthy stowaway, toward the surface via the torpedo tube. Then they struck out into the treacherous, predator-infested waters of Antarctica.

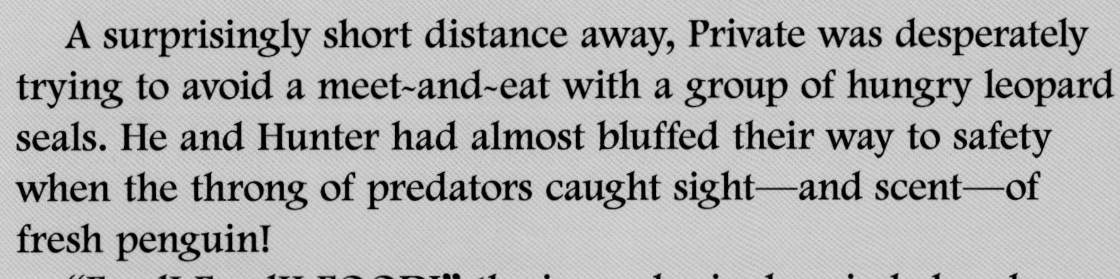

A surprisingly short distance away, Private was desperately trying to avoid a meet-and-eat with a group of hungry leopard seals. He and Hunter had almost bluffed their way to safety when the throng of predators caught sight—and scent—of fresh penguin!

"Food! Food!! FOOD!" the insanely single-minded seals all cried out at once.

Private and Hunter made a mad dash for the air hole in the ice just above their heads.

Oh, the joy of feeling solid ice beneath your flippers!

"Private, you did it! You got me home!" Hunter gushed as she took in the familiar ice floes around her. "I'll always remember you!"

"You, too!" Private said. "You take care. Don't eat anyone I wouldn't eat!"

Private watched Hunter until she was out of sight, and then he turned toward home.

"Food," said the enormous leopard seal blocking his way.

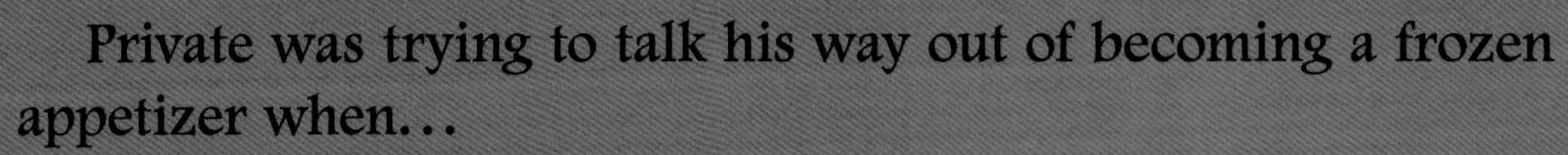

Private was trying to talk his way out of becoming a frozen appetizer when…

"Hey—Move it!—Daaaaaaddy!"

"Fuzzyface!" shouted Orson, the head seal. "Where have you been hiding?"

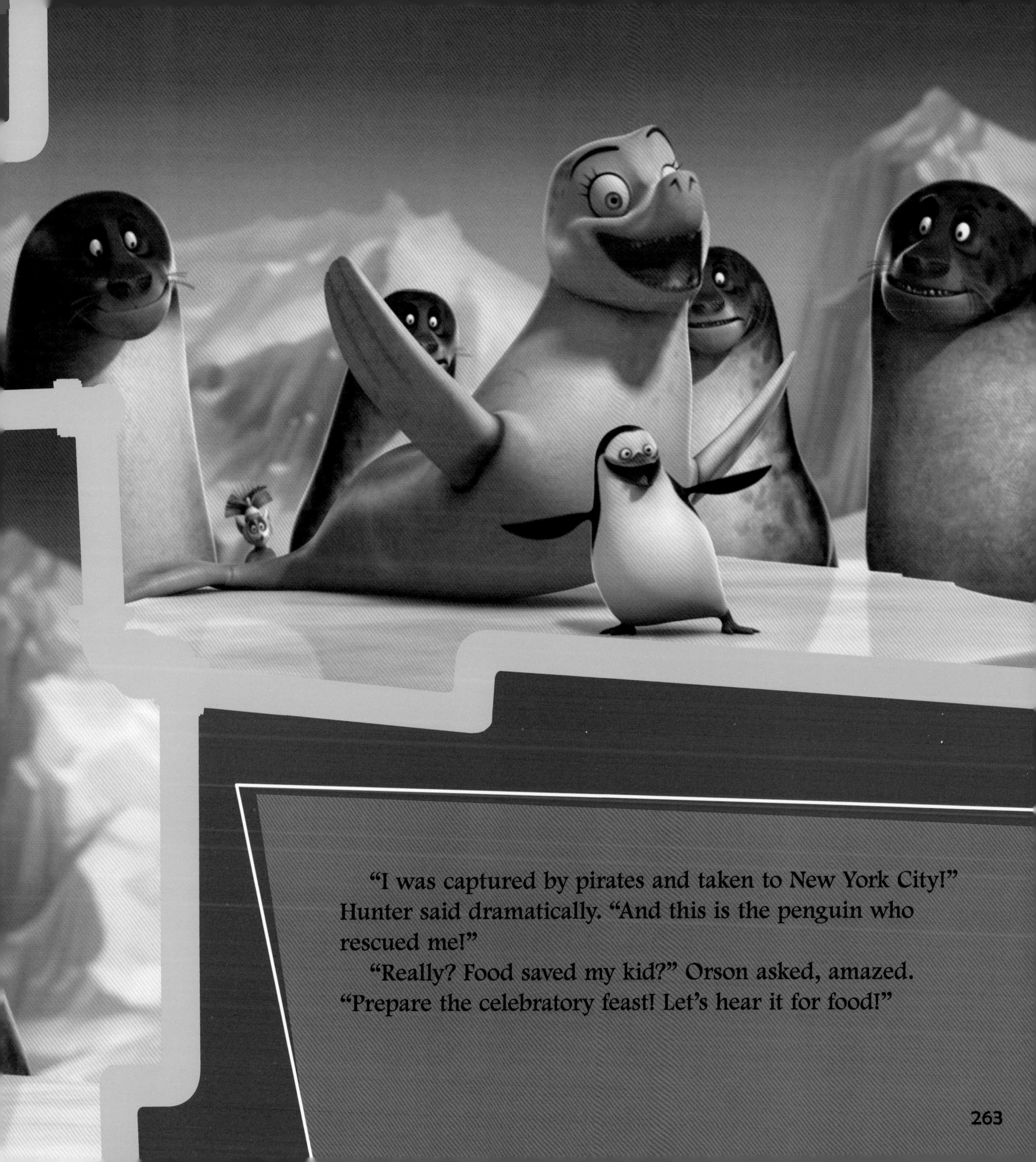

"I was captured by pirates and taken to New York City!" Hunter said dramatically. "And this is the penguin who rescued me!"

"Really? Food saved my kid?" Orson asked, amazed. "Prepare the celebratory feast! Let's hear it for food!"

Private's relief at being removed from the menu was shortlived. The celebratory feast turned out to be Skipper, Kowalski, and Rico!

"Dad, these are Private's friends!" Hunter objected.

"They rescued you, too?" Orson asked.

"Technically, they were against it," Hunter admitted reluctantly.

"Soup's on!" Orson said happily. Thinking fast, Private persuaded Orson that penguins taste better after a long, slow marinating.

Time was running out for the mostly marinated friends when Hunter took matters into her own flippers. With a quick swat, she sent them all sliding down the mountain toward freedom!

"Foooooood!" the leopard seals bellowed as they took off in hot pursuit.

"Everybody surrender!" Julien yelled, turning turncoat as the seals closed in. "Eatable ones first!"

With the seals snapping at their heels, traitorous Julien and the tasty penguins flew off an icy ramp and soared to safety!

All set to follow his friends, Private saw Orson take a disastrous tumble. The big seal was careening out of control toward cliffs of jagged ice!

Private detoured to intercept his friend's dad—and threw on the brakes. The pair skittered and skidded and finally came to a shuddering stop right at the edge of a cliff!

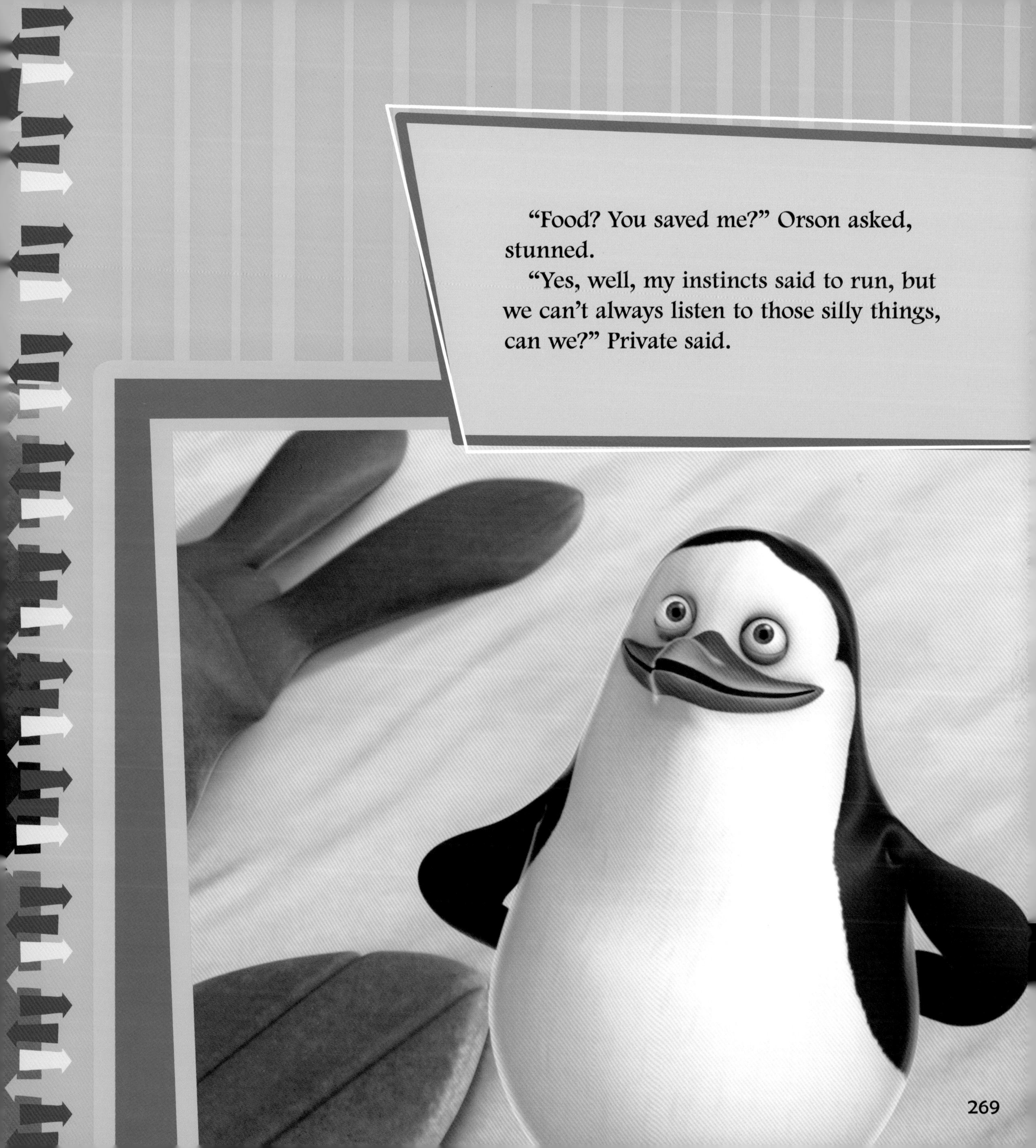

“Food? You saved me?” Orson asked, stunned.

“Yes, well, my instincts said to run, but we can’t always listen to those silly things, can we?” Private said.

"Everybody okay?" Hunter asked breathlessly. Orson looked over his daughter's shoulder at the fast-approaching seal mob.

"Go on, get him outta here," he said to Hunter.

"I'll miss you," Private said. Then he climbed trustingly into Hunter's mouth—and she tossed him to safety.

"Private, I may have misjudged that she-predator. And you," Skipper said. "If a penguin and a leopard seal can learn to get along in this crazy, mixed-up world, then maybe there's hope for all of us."

Julien snorted.

"Well," Skipper corrected, "all of us minus one."

What can I say?
Christmas looks good on me.
All I need is some mistletoe...
and Melman.

All this planning and
decorating and gift-giving.
I think I need to lie down.

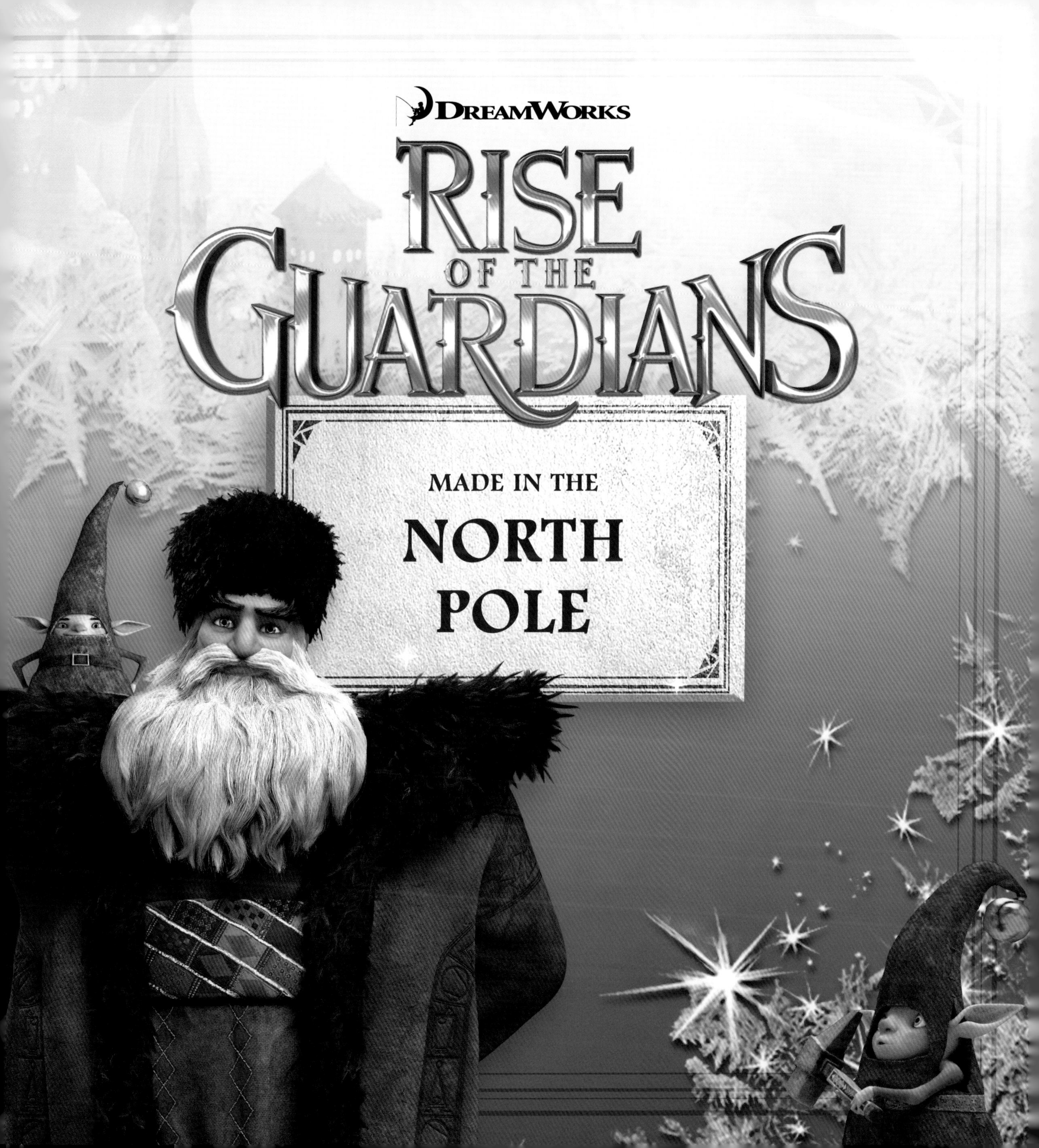
DreamWorks
RISE OF THE GUARDIANS
MADE IN THE
NORTH
POLE

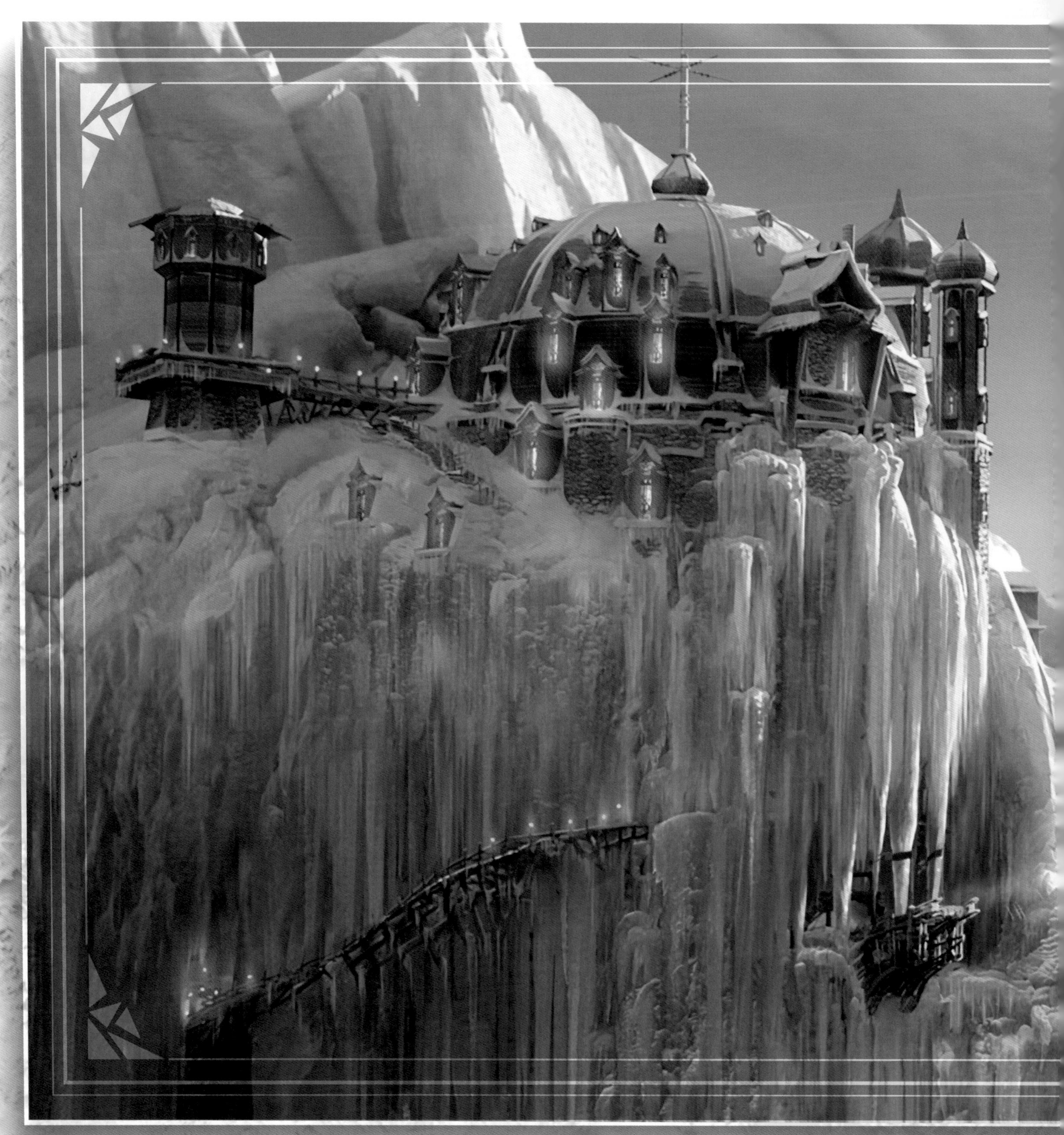

Far away, nestled deep in the icy glaciers of the North Pole, there is a hidden palace.

It's the magical place where North dreams up all of the toys that make children happy.

But North doesn't make all of the toys himself. He leads a team of Yetis and elves in his toy workshop.

Yetis are furry natives of the North Pole who guard the entrance to the palace and make all of the toys. They are loyal workers and would do anything for North! They carve, hammer, paint, and build all year long so everything's perfect for Christmas morning—even if it means repainting all the blue robots red.

Many people believe that elves build all the toys, but they are wrong. North just lets them think they're helping. What they really do is run around the factory messing things up and wrecking the Yetis' tools. Once, they even stole the Yetis' funny red hats as a joke and now they wear them every day! The hats make the elves easy to find. Follow the sound of the dangling bells and you will find an elf creating chaos in North's workshop.

The elves actually have one very important job to do: They test drive all of the toys, making sure they're fun and safe. They're very good at this job.

Every toy begins as a block of ice in North's workshop, which he carves into perfect, icy toys like trains, planes, dolls, and more.

Next, he hands the ice models to the Yetis who get to work making the real toys. Once the Yetis are done, the elves play with the toys, flying them around the room and zooming past each other to make sure they are lots of fun and won't break too easily. Soon, the finished toys are boxed and wrapped, ready to be delivered.

One of the most impressive places in North's palace is the Globe Room. The giant globe slowly spins so North can view the entire world. Each of the tiny lights on the globe is a child who believes. Green lights indicate that children are being good. Red lights indicate that children are misbehaving. But good or bad, naughty or nice, the Guardians protect them all.

The Globe Room is where the Guardians meet to make sure all the children are safe. The Man in the Moon communicates with the Guardians inside this room. It's where he tells them who will become the newest Guardian: Jack Frost.

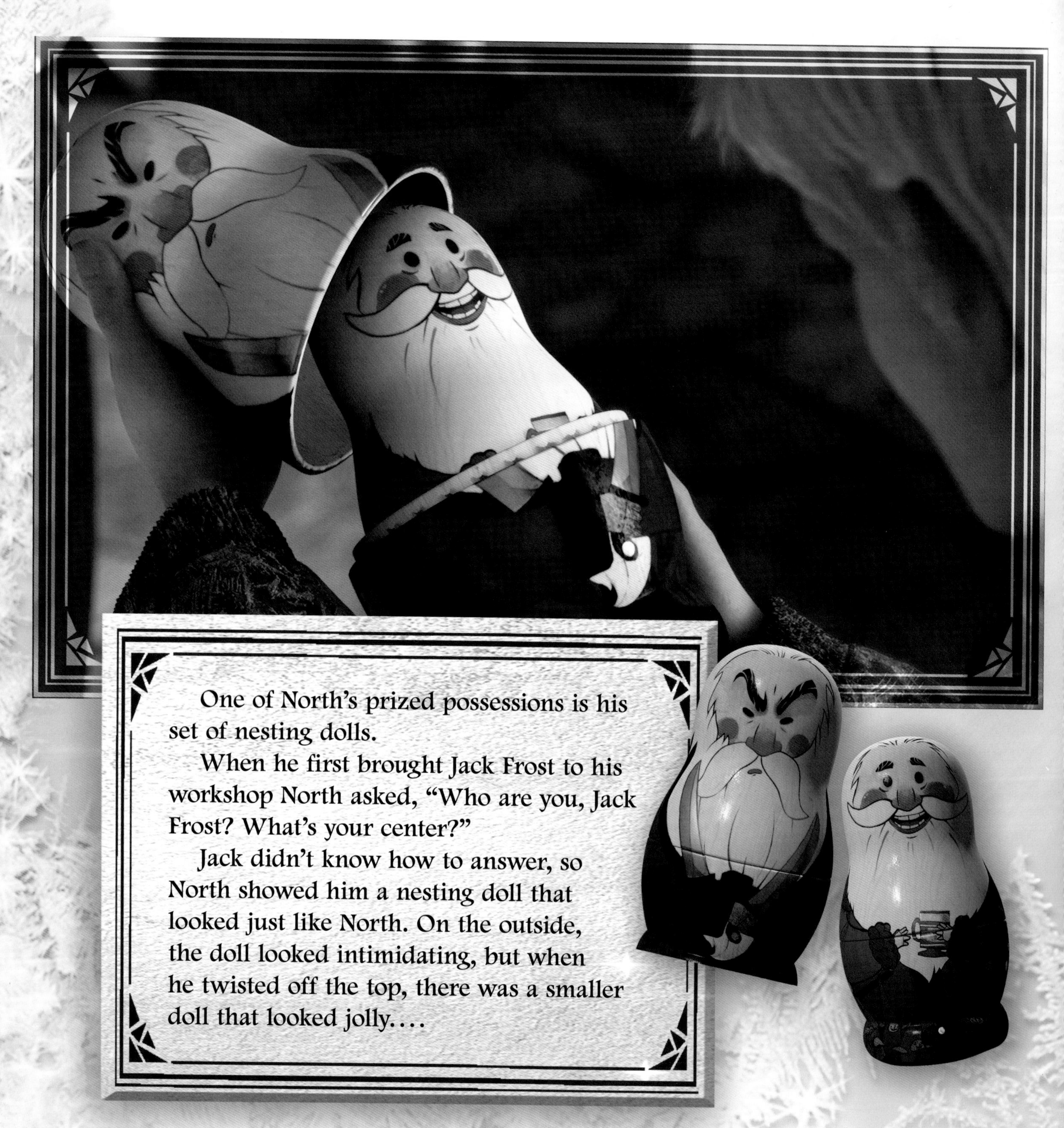

One of North's prized possessions is his set of nesting dolls.

When he first brought Jack Frost to his workshop North asked, "Who are you, Jack Frost? What's your center?"

Jack didn't know how to answer, so North showed him a nesting doll that looked just like North. On the outside, the doll looked intimidating, but when he twisted off the top, there was a smaller doll that looked jolly....

And inside there was a smaller doll that looked mysterious...
And next, an even smaller doll that looked caring.

At the very center, there was a tiny baby doll with big eyes that were full of wonder...because even though North acts tough, the truth is that he can see the wonder in everything! That's his center. That's what he protects in children. That's what makes him a Guardian.

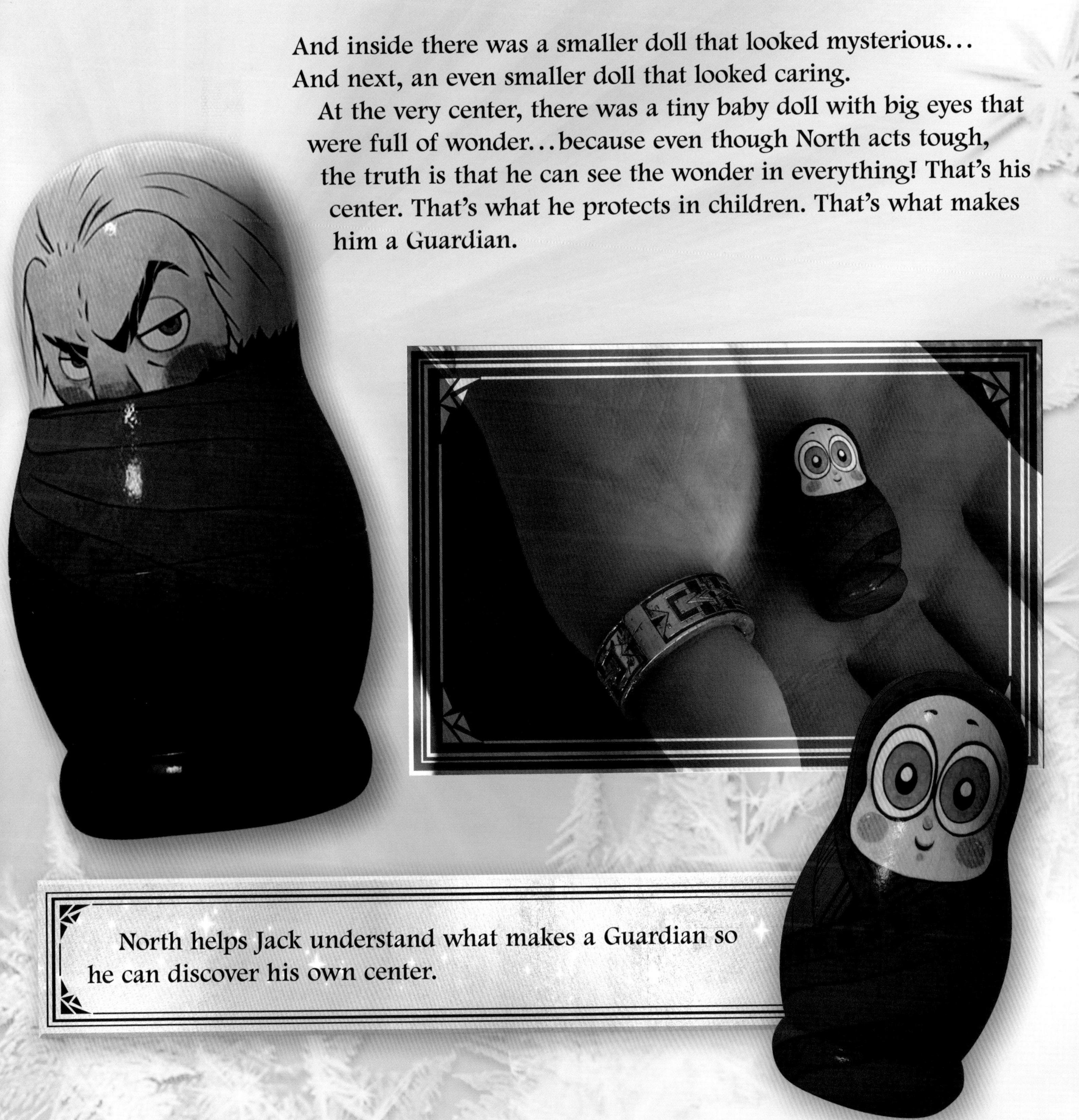

North helps Jack understand what makes a Guardian so he can discover his own center.

When it's finally time to deliver the toys, North loads up his sleigh. It's no ordinary sleigh—it's a cross between a snowmobile and a jet plane pulled by a team of powerful reindeer.

With a snap of the reins, the reindeer lift the sleigh into the air, blast from the icy mountainside, and dash through the sky with incredible speed.

Once all of the toys are delivered, the elves greet North back in his workshop with a plate of freshly baked cookies.

But there's no rest for the weary. After a few bites, it's time to start dreaming up new and exciting toys for next year!

Pulling Santa's sleigh for one night–how hard can it be?

Happy New Year to all!
But me first.